HOME FOR THE Holidays

A NOVEL

HOME FOR THE *Holidays*

A NOVEL

KATHRYN D. HULL

All rights reserved. Published by The Little Bookworm's Press. No part of this publication may be reproduced, distributed, or transmitted in any form or by any means, including photocopying, recording, or other electronic or mechanical methods, without the prior written permission of the author, except in the case of brief quotations embodied in critical reviews and certain other noncommercial uses permitted by copyright law.

Text copyright © 2024 Kathryn D. Hull
Cover/Interior Design © 2024 Kathryn D. Hull and C.T Carey
Cover Artwork used with permission from Canva
Edited by Crystal Cozza

If you purchased this book without a cover, you should be aware that this book is stolen property. It was reported as "unsold and destroyed," and neither the author nor the publisher has received any payment for this "stripped book."

This book is a work of fiction. Names, characters, places, and incidents are the product of the author's imagination or used fictitiously, and any resemblance to actual persons, living or dead, events, or locations is entirely coincidental.

ISBN: 978-1-962715-05-8

For JJ,

My candle in the window

CHAPTER ONE

Halloween

"Paige, if you don't leave right now, you're never going to make it on time," my best friend Emily said, grabbing our empty iced tea glasses and standing up. We had met for lunch at the restaurant where I worked before I headed out to my parents' house for Halloween. My parents were having everyone in the family over for dinner and pumpkin carving. The last part was my idea, which meant I kind of had to make it to the festivities on time.

"Okay, okay, I'm going," I said, following her lead and standing up. "Oof. I definitely should not have agreed to eat the rest of your fries. I might need you to roll me out of this place." I rubbed my very full stomach and made a face just to add dramatic effect. We waved over our shoulders at the hostess Kelsey, as we walked out the door to the parking lot. Emily stopped by the back of her car and dug around in her purse for her keys, while I walked to the space across from her to the back of my car and did the same.

"Text me when you get there and tell your folks and grandma I say hi. I'm sorry I can't go with you."

"Ummm, excuse me, but you cannot be sorry you are not carving pumpkins and eating Milky Ways with my family because you have a hot date with Bartender Bob. Speaking of which, I'm going to need all the deets when I get back, so please pay very good attention."

"Once again... his name is Chad... not Bob, and I promise nothing in regards to details."

I rolled my eyes as I finished unlocking my car door. "Bartender Chad does not just roll off the tongue, so until it's serious enough that I need to remember his actual name, he shall remain Bob to me. Also, don't make things worse for yourself by trying to not fill me in on details. I could request a full-scale reenactment complete with costumes and quirky accents, so really, you're getting off easy, and you should thank me..." I opened my door and started to climb in. "Oh and wear that blue sweater you just bought. Trust me!" I gave a little wave and closed the door before she had a chance to argue. I watched in the rearview mirror as she stuck her tongue out at me, and then climbed into her car.

I started my car and then grabbed my phone to check traffic and put on the appropriate driving music to keep me company on my journey. I was now running about twenty minutes later than I hoped to be, but Em and I hadn't had a proper roommate/bestie catch-up lunch in almost a week due to our current opposite work schedules, and it had been long overdue. Em worked with an event planning company and was in the middle of planning an over-the-top Sweet 16 party for a local girl and two hundred of her closest friends and family. Meanwhile, I was temporarily on evening shifts at the restaurant to help cover for the usual closing shift manager while she was on a much-needed vacation.

Once I got my 'Make a Joyful Noise' playlist playing and the appropriate route pulled up on my navigation app, I pulled out of the parking lot and headed to the freeway. I'd wait for a little while before calling my parents, just to make sure the traffic app wasn't in one of its lying moods and was indeed being honest with my current expected time of arrival.

As I drove, I thought about the next couple of days I'd spend with my family. It had been a while since we'd all gotten together, and Halloween felt like a fun excuse to do it again. I had packed prizes, so we could have pumpkin carving awards—because really, who doesn't love a little competition—as well as a couple of games we could all play.

In addition to my parents, Charles and Nancy, my sister Holly and grandparents would be there.

I knew my sister would rise to the challenge of pumpkin decorating, so I needed to bring my A-game. Coincidentally, I have not a single artistic bone in my body. Attempting anything of grandeur was, more than likely, going to be my undoing, but I would attempt it, nonetheless.

A short while later with traffic still moving at the expected pace, I would be at my parents' house in about an hour. Their house was about an hour-and-a-half from where Emily and I lived. That made it far enough away that we couldn't get together whenever we wanted without a little forethought, yet not so far that I could only see them a few times a year. I also made up for the distance by talking to them just about every single day. I opted to wait a few more minutes before calling my dad with my ETA, content to have some quiet time just for me. It had been an incredibly busy week at work, and I was thankful to have the next couple of days off.

Most days I loved my job, or at least the people I worked with and the people I met. Most of the time, that was enough for me, but lately, the long shifts and ever-changing hours were really starting to feel draining. At the restaurant, every employee gets to prioritize one day of the week that is important to them for whatever reason, but beyond that preference, all bets were off when it came to scheduling.

I always kept Sundays as my preference, to ensure I could always get to church, and was grateful that part of my life could stay consistent and prioritized. Aside from Sundays, though, I tried to be as available and flexible as possible for my boss.

I called home when I was about fifteen minutes away. Traffic had been moving really well, and I had gotten a little carried away in my impromptu solo concert. I tried reaching each of my parents on their cell phones. Knowing I wouldn't get my mom because she could never hear the stupid thing ring, I tried her first anyways, thinking that one of these days she'd learn to put the phone on vibrate so she could at least feel it. It rang five times before heading to voicemail. Today was apparently not that day.

Next, I tried my dad. He was usually a given. I think he would shower with his phone if he had a handy place to set it. To my surprise, his phone also went to voicemail after several rings. Peculiar, I thought to myself. If I didn't get my dad, it was usually not that he didn't answer, but that he dropped the phone, or pushed a wrong button with his thumb. "Who makes these damn buttons so freaking touchy?" he'd always ask, as I'd get hung up on. Oddly enough, being hung up on, repeatedly, by one's father does not give a girl the complex you'd think it should.

I tried the house next. After the third ring, the phone was finally picked up, but not by either of my parents. It was my sister, Holly. "Hey, where are you?" she asked after I told her I was, "Me."

"I'm on my way. I got held up at work... sort of. That's a lie. I was having lunch and being led astray by garlic parmesan fries and fresh brewed iced tea. I was powerless against their allure. Feel bad for me." She laughed, used to my antics. I continued, "What are you doing there already?"

"Mom and Dad were running late with Grandma, so they asked if I would come over a little early to take care of the dogs. Mom sounded a little weird on the phone, so Ben and I came right over. They should be here any second."

"Weird how? Like something is wrong with Grandma?" I asked, getting a little nervous. My grandmother had been living up north with my Uncle Derrick and Aunt Charlotte until earlier this year. Then, after getting admitted into the hospital, saying her final goodbyes to her sons, and scaring all of us half to death, she decided God and my Grandpa

Jimmy weren't ready for her to join them in Heaven just yet, and moved back home near my parents. It was great having her back to where we could visit her, but I was prepared to give her a stern talking to if she ever pulled a stunt like that again!

"No, Grandma's fine, I made sure. Apparently, she has some big news she wants to tell all of us tonight. Dad was trying to get it out of her, but she wasn't budging at all. Mom just sounded like... well, like she didn't like not knowing the news."

"Maybe she met a man in her senior complex and they are running away to elope!" I said. "There is that ladies' man, Ron something or other, that has flirted with her at Happy Hour."

"Is that the guy that wears his shirts disturbingly unbuttoned and uses way too much pomade... which, in my opinion, is any amount of pomade?" my sister asked.

"That's the guy! Hey! If they do elope, I could ask Emily to make tiny pomade party favors!" I was just about to exit the freeway, and it was nice to have my sister keeping me company on the phone, even if we were talking about nothing. No way would my Grandma Jane ever elope, especially with a man who took longer to get ready than she did.

"Grandpa Ron... Ronald? Ronnie? It could catch on," she said.

I heard our family's three dachshunds begin to bark in the background. Once they got going, it was impossible to get them to shut up. There was a tin can that contained a handful of pennies that could be used to shake at them when they were getting too rambunctious, but it turns out it is even more annoying to us human folk than it is to the dogs. My parents didn't just have two daughters anymore. Ever since the trio of dachshunds, Dickens, Oliver, and Nicholas—I say if you are going to name your dogs after characters from literature, you may as well pick the literary giants—joined the family, my sister and I had to compete with our furry four-legged brothers for our parents' attention. Sometimes we thought they were totally winning.

"They must be home. I'll tell them you are close but get your butt here now! I want to know the big news!" Holly said, and then hung up. I wasn't sure I wanted to hear the big news, and frankly, would probably have been much happier waiting until everyone else heard the news to determine—by the looks on their faces—whether or not I wanted to hear the news at all. I have always known that I was gifted with an overactive imagination, which I frequently use to work myself into a tizzy about absolutely nothing realistic, but I really don't want a Grandpa Ronnie.

I drove the rest of the way wondering what on earth my Grandma Jane could want to tell us that we all needed to be in the same room to hear. When I pulled up to the traffic light on my parents' street, I fired off a quick text to Emily, letting her know I arrived safely. I may have also reminded her that the pink lipstick that really makes her blue eyes pop was in my makeup drawer in the bathroom of our apartment... again, just in case.

I had to send the message to Emily before actually arriving at my parents' house, because once you get down the street to the house itself, there is absolutely no cell phone reception. Well, with the few exceptions in the following locations: the master bathroom, on the small end table to the left of the big couch, in the right-hand top corner of my bed if the phone is turned at a ninety-degree angle, or while standing on the second to the top stair, but only if the lights are out and you rock back and forth.

As I pulled into the driveway, my father was standing outside waiting for me, as he usually does in order to help me pull my car into the garage. They have one of those three car garages where the third spot is really like a half a spot and mostly used for extra storage or a gym. My mini cooper fits wonderfully in that spot, so my dad has to keep the area clean, just for my arrival. I like to think I'm contributing to the overall organization of his man-cave by not allowing junk to take over that little nook. I also liked to tell my dad the builders made it just for me, since I—as his youngest daughter—deserve things like that. He liked to remind me that he hates both clutter and working out, so really it was inevitability more than a purposeful decision. I would then wink at him, letting him know it was okay, that he had to say things like that so Holly wouldn't get jealous, but that I knew the truth.

Instead of pulling me into the garage with a quick wave like he normally would, my dad pointed down to the ground, repeatedly, in a firm motion. I took this to mean roll down the window, although I suppose looking back on it, he could have been telling me to duck, or anything else really that one could determine by the simple gesture of pointing down.

"Just park Phoebe here." Yes, I'm the girl who names her car something super cute, and then doesn't allow anyone to refer to her as an 'it' ever again. "We'll pull her in the garage later. We have to get inside. Grandma Jane has done something... well, I'll let her tell you herself," my dad said, opening my car door before I had actually even stopped fully.

"She finally got a tattoo? What's it of?" I asked. It's not my fault that I was born with a sarcasm gene that just won't quit. I like to think of myself as the Lorelei Gilmore of the real world, armed and ready with a witty comeback to be delivered at a moment's notice.

"Butter Bean, a tattoo might have been a better idea. See if you can talk her into that instead," my dad said. From the look on his face, I could tell he was at least partly kidding. That was a good sign, wasn't it? I mean if he still had his sense of humor, the world couldn't be coming to an end just yet.

"Give me five minutes and a computer. We can find the perfect one... Seriously Dad, is it bad?" I asked, finally losing steam on the joke train. "Is she ok?" I climbed out of the car, forgetting all about my laundry basket and duffle bag in the back, locked the car door and followed my dad to the garage door.

"She's fine. Physically at least. Mentally, right now, the jury is still out. She's made... an investment of sorts," my dad said.

"What kind of investment could she have possibly made?" I asked, hoping he would give me a bit more. "Holly said Grandma wanted to tell us all at once. I'm guessing that 'us' didn't include Granddaughter Paige?" I was halfway relieved that everyone knew and could now help me digest the information a bit better, and halfway miffed that I was excluded from the initial information reveal. What can I say? I'm a complicated person.

"Mom and I got it out of her when we were at her apartment. When we got here, we needed to call Uncle

Simon and Uncle Derrick and get them involved. This decision was hers to make... which she has reminded us of several times throughout the past hour, but it's going to affect all of us. Holly and Ben found out because they were listening in on the group phone call."

"Well, geez, can you tell me already? Before you open that door and I get bombarded by everyone else's opinion?" I said, blocking the door. I might have been the last to know, but that didn't mean I couldn't at least be prepared a little.

"Grandma Jane bought some property. More specifically, she bought a bed and breakfast..."

"She did WHAT?" I said, not allowing my dad to finish. "How... where... why??? How can she buy an entire hotel? She doesn't do things like that! She doesn't just spend money on anything, let alone a freakin' hotel!" My head was spinning. My grandmother was very careful with... frankly everything. She didn't make out of the blue, non-calculated decisions, especially when it came to finances. She was responsible with her money, and she certainly never, ever, just threw it away on a whim. She even gambled on a budget, which I found incredibly odd, yet responsible.

"She has her reasons, and she wanted to be able to explain it to everyone, without prejudgment. You can imagine how well that is going in this family right now. We better get in there. When I left, your uncles were asking about an escape clause in the sale of the property while Grandma looked like she was getting ready to just turn off her hearing aid and stop listening." He opened the door and we walked inside. We were not greeted by the three barking amigos, as was customary in this house. It would seem that even they got the message that now was not the time for fun and games, and they should draw as little attention to themselves as possible.

I decided to take my cues from the dogs, figuring that quiet, low to the ground, and out of the way might be my best approach while I tried to wrap my brain around all of the information I had just been given. Didn't anyone realize I just wanted a little pumpkin carving, maybe a few pieces of candy, and perhaps a not-so-scary Halloween themed movie?

"Paige is here," my mom announced from the kitchen table where everyone was gathered around. I couldn't tell if it was more for the people who were talking animatedly on the other end of the phone, or for my grandmother, but I tried to give her the 'I'm with the dogs, leave me out of it' look. It turns out that is not a commonly translated look, which is probably why she didn't catch on and continued to pull out a chair while pointing at it, indicating I should sit down. What was with my family suddenly pointing at everything to communicate with me?

I walked over to the table and kissed my grandma on the cheek as she sat calmly stoic with her arms crossed loosely in her lap. The look of patience and confidence on her face was one that I had grown up knowing to mean that she was in control of the situation at hand. This was incredibly reassuring in the few moments of complete silence following my mom's declaration of my arrival, because it meant that my grandmother was firm in her decision, even if we didn't understand it yet. So, I figured I owed it to her to at least hear her out without making too many judgments on my own. After all, isn't that the only thing she'd asked from us in regard to the news? I could give her that.

"Boy, do you know how to spice up a party!" I said into her ear and then smiled at her so she would hopefully know at least one of us was ready to listen to the whys of her decision.

My sister seemed to also be oddly calm at the information. I became suspicious of this immediately. I love my sister greatly, but I also know that she loves a good soap opera style drama, especially when she wasn't involved in the creation of it. She smiled at me from her Zen like state, and I immediately mouthed the words "What is going on?" to which my soon to be brother-in-law—God bless him—responded to by silently sliding over a freshly poured glass of wine to my side of the table, and then raised his own glass in a 'Drink up, because you are going to need it' kind of way. I love my brother-in-law.

About an hour and a half after my arrival, the group phone call finally came to an end. Here was what came out of it. First, Grandma Jane was, most definitely, not un-buying the property. She had known exactly what she was doing when she purchased it—I told you so—and she intended to keep it.

Second, I learned that the property was close to where my parents, sister, grandmother, and other grandparents, Rose and Frank, lived. It sits on a hill, has fifteen guest rooms, and had been a bed and breakfast since the early 1900s. My grandmother had seen the property once while driving home from lunch with my father, not thinking much of it other than it was a beautiful Victorian style mansion with a 'For Sale' sign out front and a lovely garden. A few weeks later, she read an article about the history of the mansion, as well as why it was being sold and she remembered again how beautiful she had thought it was that day.

This led to the third piece of information... why she bought it in the first place. The answer to this piece of the puzzle was... wait for it... all of us. Apparently, my grandmother had a dream about the B&B—that's what all the cool kids call them, B&Bs—and in that dream, her entire family was there, gathered together. When she woke, she knew it was something she needed to make a reality.

She reminded her sons that this was something she had always wanted. Her father had owned his own restaurant when she was growing up. As a child that had inspired her to want to own something of her own. That by doing so, she would be able to give her family a legacy, something that could be passed down from generation to generation.

At this point in the conversation, I decided it would be a good time to remind my grandma that, although the idea seemed lovely, none of us actually knew the first thing about running a bed and breakfast. That in order to pass it down from generation to generation, it would have to be successful enough to survive that long. Apparently my tidbit of insight did nothing to dissuade her, because she continued on with her planning. It did, however, lead us to the final piece of knowledge, and the biggest shocker of all.

She wanted me to help get the B&B settled and open for business. Yes, me. I don't know exactly how she came to this decision, but she let us know that she felt this was something that everyone could have a hand in. My dad could help with some of the maintenance, my mom, the interior decorating. My sister could help ensure that we were up to code on all safety issues, Uncle Derrick could do all the signage for the place, and I could organize and run the front desk. She was also hoping that Emily would be able to help me. And the best part? We would need the place to be ready by the first of the year because the previous owners had already booked the hotel for January, and my grandma doesn't want to turn the guests away.

While I sat there with my mouth open, and no words to describe the shock that I felt, my mother was kind enough to jump in. "Mom, we all have jobs! There is no way that we would have time to work our full-time jobs and meet that kind of deadline!"

"Paige can do it. I will pay her salary," my grandmother said in her very matter of fact tone.

"Grandma, I have a job. And I don't live anywhere near here! I have a whole life back home. With friends, and bills, and responsibilities. And I have no idea how to do any of this!" I would have continued to ramble on in the very non-matter-of-fact manner in which I currently seemed accustomed to, but she cut me off.

"You don't want to do your job forever; you've said so yourself. Do you even like it? If it turns out that you really do, work with your boss to ensure that it will still be there once we are up and running, if you'd still like to go back. I will pay you what you currently make, including tips, and you can live here with your parents for a little while, if they approve. You could eventually move into the guest house at the back of the property, if you'd rather have your own space. I think that just about sums up your whole life as you put it. Your friends, if they are the type of people worth keeping in your life, will be supportive. As I mentioned earlier, I have a role for Emily to play in all of this, if she chooses, so you'd still have best friend time."

By now, everyone was channeling their inner dachshund because the entire room had fallen silent. I believe we were feeling some sort of communal shock and weren't sure how to process what we'd all just heard. While there were a thousand thoughts, and fragments of thoughts, running through my head, the external world was incredibly quiet. My mind, with all of its 'Who does she think she is? I can't just leave my job and my life to move back home to my parents' house... Emily is just starting to really make a name for herself, why would she want to leave? Can I actually, maybe, really make this work? Do I even like my job enough to stay?' was loud enough to be a twelve-piece symphony playing a robust concerto. I couldn't be certain, but there was also a reasonable chance that my mouth had frozen in the open position.

My mother was beginning to turn an interesting shade of pink, which let me know that she was feeling the same intense shock I was but was travelling down the angry path of emotions. My sister seemed to be matching my mother in coloring, but she was also physically gripping the table to keep herself still. There was an uncomfortable silence from the other end of the phone, and I could feel that at any moment someone's dam was going to break, and things were going to get said that could never be taken back.

God must have sensed the tension in the room and sent some angelic little ghosts and goblins to rescue me, because all of the sudden the doorbell rang, snapping us out of the tense silence we were all in. "That must be the first trick-

or-treaters," my father said, without moving a muscle, or blinking for that matter.

My mother got up to answer the door, which I think was probably the best choice for her to make at the moment. It gave her an opportunity to either take a breath and collect her thoughts, or fully digest the information and blow her top when she came back into the room.

I finally emerged from my state of shock enough to somehow regain my motor skills and get my mouth working again. I looked over to my dad, seeing if I could make eye contact. My goal was to get him, and my sister, to back me up, then to speak calmly and rationally. My dad met my eyes. I smiled a half smile at him, then nodded my head to let him know that I was okay. Alright, maybe not okay, but at least in control of all of my faculties. I then looked over to my sister and stared at her until she looked at me. I subtly shook my head no, indicating that she shouldn't say anything at that point.

"Okay... here's what I think," I said, breaking the silence. "Grandma, this is obviously something that everyone is going to have to digest for a bit before anything else is discussed. We aren't going to get any further tonight." I looked around the room to see if everyone was listening but didn't stop to allow anyone to break into my train of thought. "I think that it is safe to assume that if you have put this much thought into what exactly you think all our roles in this whole thing should be, that you have also thought of a backup plan in case we didn't go along with it. If you haven't, I think that your job is to do so before we go too much further down this path."

My mom came back into the room and following behind her were her parents, my other grandparents, who must have been briefly filled in because they came into the room and didn't seem at all surprised by what they saw. A couple of people opened their mouths to jump in, but I wouldn't allow it.

I continued, "No wait, I want to finish. The information given tonight affects us all, but right now it seems to affect me more than the rest of you, so I think I should be the one to voice my opinion. So, here's the bottom line. We all came together tonight to spend Halloween as a family, and that is what I would like to do. I don't want to talk about this anymore right now. I will at some point, but not right now. I am going upstairs to drop off my bag and change, then I am coming back down to start carving pumpkins.

"If anyone would like to join me, I would love it. I have some thinking that I need to do, but right now is not the time or place for it. Uncle Derrick, Uncle Simon, I hope you guys have a great Halloween." And with that, to my own surprise, I stood up, grabbed my car keys, then headed back towards the garage. I needed out of the room. I needed oxygen. I needed a moment alone.

I grabbed my bags from the car to take to my room. Once I was back inside my sister followed me up the stairs to check whether I was okay or not. "I cannot believe that she had the nerve to..." Holly started, but I held up my hand.

"I know everyone has their own opinion, but I really don't want to talk about it, Hol. I don't want to think about it right now." I told her, keeping my voice steady. "I just want to get through tonight."

"Well, are you even going to consider what she said? I think it's ridiculous! You have a job that you have worked hard at for years! How could she possibly think you would just walk away from that?" She flopped down on my bed. I began to change into something more comfortable.

"I don't know if I'm going to think about it. I don't know anything right now except that I want to go downstairs, carve a freakin' pumpkin, and pass out candy!" I threw my clothes on the bed with more force than necessary. I was finally getting angry. "I want to follow the plan that we had for tonight and pretend like this conversation never happened. I don't want any more complications right now! And I REALLY DON'T WANT TO TALK ABOUT THIS!"

I realized I was yelling by the last sentence, but I didn't care. I wanted to be alone for a few minutes. I wanted to run away, to think and to have some time to pray. I wanted to fast forward the day, and I wanted to rewind it so that the news my grandma gave us never happened. I couldn't do any of those things. I was spinning.

I stood back up and began heading back downstairs. My sister followed. "So, what now?" she asked, trying to figure out what I needed most.

"Now we carve a freaking pumpkin, even if it kills us," I said, determined that even if it took all night, I would have the best pumpkin anyone on this block had ever seen. As long as my hands were busy, maybe my brain didn't have to be.

The doorbell rang again as we reached the bottom of the stairs. "I'll get it!" I called into the other room, where there was still some sort of conversation happening, but in hushed tones.

"Trick-or-Treat!" I opened the door as a ballerina, witch, clown, Darth Vader, and adorable puppy dog recited in enthusiastic unison. I gave them each a giant handful of candy, that I am sure my mom would object to, and grabbed a bag of fun-size Skittles out for myself.

"Trick." I replied, "Definitely trick. You guys have no idea."

CHAPTER TWO

The Morning After

The ballet teacher was yelling. Not at me, of course. I was doing my pliés with gusto and proper form, just like I was supposed to. She was yelling at Darth Vader. He was having trouble getting low enough to the ground for her liking. I thought his uniform could be a major part of the encumbrance but didn't feel the need to draw attention to myself by saying so. While the ballet teacher was small enough to barely come up below his chest and weighed practically nothing, she was still terrifying. She insisted his issues were all in his mind. Funny, I thought to myself, because he could probably use his mind to do so much more than ballet.

The giggle that slipped out of my throat made the teacher turn back towards me. She opened her mouth to give me a firm scolding, but instead, she started singing. Or rather chirping. Like a cell phone. It was absolutely disturbing. And annoying. How could I politely tell her to stop? She did not stop. Instead, she walked slowly in my direction and only got louder, repeating the same sixteen chords over. And over. And over, and over again. Her face was completely deadpan, but her sound kept getting more and more exuberant.

My eyes flew open. I felt around the top corner of my bed, where my phone usually sat to charge, and started rapidly tapping the screen anywhere I could in the hopes of making the stupid thing shut up. I blinked rapidly until my eyes could start to focus on the small screen to see what time it was, and who had the audacity to not turn off my alarm. Me. I was the one who had that audacity. The screen read 6:15 am. I had gotten exactly three hours of sleep. My dream came flooding back to me, and strangely enough it made me simultaneously worried about my sanity and have a strong desire to go take a barre class. "Serves me right for that seventh pack of sour Skittles at two o'clock in the morning."

I closed my eyes again for a few more minutes, mentally reliving Mr. Vader's terrible port de bras, blissfully unaware of the events that had transpired the night before. It didn't take long before it all came flooding back though, making me wish life was filled with more absurd moments involving Lord Vader in a tutu, and less absurd moments involving my grandmother making crazy life-changing, family-dividing decisions.

I pulled my covers closer to my chin and picked up my phone. I flipped it to my alarm setting to make sure that I had disabled it instead of just hitting snooze, which has happened too many times for my liking, then dialed Emily's number. She picked up on the fourth ring, right before it went to voicemail. "Are you dead?" she asked, groggily.

"Don't be ridiculous, I wouldn't be calling you if I was dead... I would just stop on by in ghost form," I answered.

"Are you in jail?"

"Not currently."

"Is it early enough that I'm going to hang up on you if I open my eyes?"

"That depends entirely on what time zone I choose to base my answer on," I said. I felt pretty safe from the threat of a hang up. If it was something she was planning on doing, I was fairly confident, based on the historical fact that she would have done it already, and not exerted the extra energy into asking the second or third question. "But how about I tell you why I called. And then, after you fix everything, because you are amazing, I'll tell you what time it is? That way it'll be later, and you'll never have to know." No reason to push my luck too far.

"Uggh..." was her response. In early morning Em language, that particular form of grunt translated loosely into something like, "Go right ahead. Tell me everything, I'm all ears." So, I did. I told her all about the night before. I didn't leave anything out because, well frankly if I couldn't freak out with her, who the heck could I freak out with?

When I finished, the other end was silent. So silent, I began to think that I either got disconnected from her a while ago and just didn't notice, which would suck because then I'd have to start all over again, which I really didn't want to do, or that she fell asleep on me, which again, boo for the starting over, and way to take my non-mid-life crisis seriously, Snoozer!

"Ummm... hello?" I asked into the phone, hoping that somehow the strange silence that we all experienced last night was just contagious.

"I'm here."

"And?"

"Digesting."

"Any luck you'll be digested in the next five minutes?"

"No. Why?"

"I need to visit the little Bed-And-Breakfast-Setter-Upper's room."

"Go to the bathroom."

"Want me to call you back?"

"I'll call you."

"K. Are you kind of wishing now that I had called you from jail instead?"

"Meh. Maybe. I'll let you know when I see the amount of paperwork involved... Seriously though, don't freak out. Or at least give yourself an appropriate amount of designated freak out time, and then relax. Go do something fun. Take a yoga class... oooh! Or maybe a barre class or something. You've always wanted to try that. We'll figure it out." Okay... creepy about the whole barre thing, there Jedi Master Em... but at least she did get that I was on the verge of changing my name and moving to a yurt in the middle of Nowheresville USA. That was a good sign.

"Pro/Con list?" I asked.

"It definitely couldn't hurt."

"K."

"Bye."

"Bye, friend."

That was it. The shortest, least informative conversation I had been a part of since I had arrived at my parent's house, and yet it was the one that made me feel most at ease—except for the whole barre class mind meld creepiness. I hung up the phone and climbed out of bed quietly. My parents were probably awake already, but there was a chance they were still curled up in bed. I wasn't quite ready to talk to them yet. I opened my door slowly and peeked around it. Their door was closed. I tiptoed to the bathroom so the dogs wouldn't hear me and start to bark, and then back to my room to grab my Bible and journal before tiptoeing downstairs. I was not going to be able to go back to sleep, even if I wanted to, so coffee and quiet time was my next biggest priority.

After getting the pot of coffee started, I set out my favorite autumn mug and creamer, grabbed a blanket from the blanket basket next to the fireplace, turned on one of the living room lights, and found the remote control that started the gas fireplace. I poured the fresh, hot coffee and creamer in my mug, grabbed my Bible and journal then curled up on the couch.

About twenty minutes later, I heard my parents' door open and several pairs of tiny little paws excitedly running down the stairs before being greeted by my three furry little brothers. My mom was not far behind, wrapped in her robe and wearing slippers. She waved a good morning, trying to not disturb my journaling, before heading outback so the dogs could do their morning business. When they were finished, she came back in, grabbed another festive fall mug, and poured herself some of the deliciously hot brew.

"How did you sleep?" Mom asked, heading to the oversized chair next to the couch and curling up in it.

"Not much really. Fine enough when I did though. Weird dreams."

"Candy before bed?"

"Sour skittles. You and Daddy been up talking about last night's events?"

"A little..." my mom said, as we both turned our attention to the stairs where my dad had just come down into the room.

"Good morning. Coffee smells great," my dad said.

"Help yourself, and come on over," I said, closing my journal and setting it down on the end table on top of my Bible and picking up my mug. "Would you mind giving me a little warm up while you're at it please?" I said, smiling innocently up at him as he came over to take my mug from me.

"I was telling your mom something that Grandma Jane told me last night when I was driving her home. She said she didn't mention it in front of all of us because she didn't think it was the right time," my dad said as he poured his coffee, then mine and headed into the living room to sit down with us.

I sat up straighter and crisscross-apple-sauced my legs as I took the mug from where my dad stood offering it to me. "What did she say?" I asked, taking a sip of the now-perfect-temperature-coffee.

"She mentioned that there was more to it when she shared with everyone last night about her dream."

"What did she say?" My mom and I both asked at the same time.

My dad nodded his head yes and took a sip of his drink. "That what she told everyone about the dream was true, but she said it was different than her usual dreams. She said it was more real than any dreams she usually had. She said you would understand what she meant by that, Paige."

Both my parents looked at me for some sort of explanation. I took a deep breath trying to figure out how to put it into words for my parents, because I did know exactly what my grandma was trying to tell me. In my family, faith had been something that had always been on the edges of our lives, but never firmly in the center. It was something everyone knew existed, but growing up, it was not part of our everyday lives. I had a curiosity about God and Jesus for as long as I could remember, and my faith had grown and changed over time as I explored and learned. It had taken me until a few years prior, in my early thirties, to really find myself and my faith. Everyone in my family now knew it was a huge part of who I am, but they were not in the same place as me, except for my Grandma Rose. She knows exactly who she is in her faith as well, and I am grateful for that example.

I had told my Grandma Jane once about a dream that I had before I was baptized. That the dream had been so vivid and clear when I woke up, I knew that the dream itself was more than just my brain or imagination, but that there was a message in it that I was meant to hear. The next week I followed through, renewed my faith, and got baptized. My Grandma Jane knew how much it took for me to tell her that story, precisely because we didn't have a track record of talking about faith, and it was something I was starting to lead the charge in with the family. She told me once how much she admired my bravery, for being willing to be vulnerable with her and with the rest of the family.

My parents were both still looking at me and waiting for an explanation. I sighed and let the mug warm my hands. I still sometimes felt awkward talking about these things with my family, in case they mistook my real experiences as crazy talk. "I told Grandma about a dream I had that helped me cement my decision on getting baptized again as an adult. How the dream had felt different... more real somehow... and I just knew it was more than a dream. That's what she was talking about." I stared into my coffee before taking another sip, indicating that no further questions on the subject would be taken at this time. I took us back to the conversation at hand, "So, did she say anything else about what was in the dream?"

"She said Grandpa Jimmy was there at the bed and breakfast with her, and they were having tea. He'd come to visit and brought a friend with him. The friend was Laurie..." my dad trailed off, waiting for my reaction. In all fairness to him, it was a solid idea to pause for a moment because I choked on the coffee I had just put in my mouth and needed a moment to be able to remember how to swallow and breathe, instead of spitting it out.

"Laurie? As in Emily's mom, Laurie?" I asked, shocked. Of all the names that I could have expected to come out of my grandmother's mouth, Laurie Nettle was not anywhere on the list. Laurie was like a second mother to me, since Em and I had been best friends for over a decade. Late last year, Laurie had been diagnosed with cancer, and it was an aggressive form. She passed away earlier this year. It wasn't so much that Laurie had made an appearance in a dream that caught me off-guard; Em, her sister Heidi, myself, and even my mom had often dreamed of her since her passing. What made it odd was that my grandmother had only met Laurie one time before she passed.

"Yes. She said Grandpa Jimmy kept gushing over the property and telling her how proud he was that she was finally doing something to realize her dream. As they continued to talk, he became insistent that Grandma meet his friend, because she had something important that she needed to tell her. When Laurie came in and sat with them, she gave Grandma a piece of advice. She said 'Life is too short. It's our job as mothers to lead the way, because they don't always know what is best for them.' The family creating a legacy... something that they could build and grow together was a gift that would change their lives and the lives of everyone who came to stay there." My dad paused again to let everything sink in while he took another sip of his coffee.

"Grandma said that when she woke up, she knew that the dream wasn't just a dream, and she needed to buy the property."

I sat quietly for a minute, surprise still washing over me. I didn't think anything could shock me more than the information the night before, but it turned out I was wrong. Despite that fact, I felt a smile creep on my face. Laurie

Nettle. That woman was such a dynamic spirit. She was never afraid to tell anyone exactly what she thought, especially if she believed it was what was best for them. She was a force unlike any I had known before her, with a heart of gold and a generous spirit. I had no doubt in my mind that if she felt the need, she would bust into my grandma's dream and deliver the message she needed to.

Laurie had this beautifully creative and adventurous mind, and if she were still here with us, she would be the first one on board with this crazy plan my grandmother had concocted. I am lucky enough to still catch glimpses of her in both of her daughters. I couldn't explain it to my parents in a way they would understand in that moment, but I knew that if Grandma Jane had seen both Grandpa Jimmy and Laurie in that bed and breakfast in the way my dad had described, that it was indeed more than just a dream... It was something that I needed to pay attention to.

I still couldn't say for sure that I thought any of this was a good idea, but I think that was the first moment where I realized I had a role to play in making my grandma's dream—pun intended—a reality. I still had no idea exactly how any of it was going to work, or what that role was, but if Grandma had Laurie and Grandpa Jimmy on her side, then I was going to need to have a long conversation with God because He was definitely up to something.

"I need pancakes," I announced to the room. Both my parents looked at me like I'd finally cracked as I stood up and started folding the blanket that I'd been curled under.

"Pancakes? That's what you have to say to everything your father just told you?" My mom said in disbelief. Clearly my parents were not on the same train of thought I was on, and it was rapidly leaving the station.

"I don't have all the answers, Mom. There is a lot to think about, and to pray about... and eventually to talk more about. But right now, I know that if Grandpa and Laurie came to visit, something is happening here. And that means we need all our brain power to help figure this out. And my brain has just informed me that in order to participate in today's activities, it requires pancakes. I have a sneaky suspicion your brain feels the exact same way. Besides, I trusted Laurie's opinion when she stood in front of me in all her flesh and blood and 'limited view of the world' glory, so why would I change that now that she has a front row to the bigger picture?" I smiled and then said, "Why? Do you have something against pancakes?"

"I like pancakes," my dad said, standing up in solidarity with me. I nodded my approval.

"Now you have to come, cause its two against one," I said, reaching out a hand, offering to help pull my mom out of her chair.

"She's right, Nancy. Besides, it's incredibly difficult to argue logic that you cannot follow, especially on an empty stomach, so at least this way we have some sort of a plan. I vote pancakes and then we can tackle the subject of your-grandmother-wants-you-to-quit-your-job-move-back-home-with-your-parents-and-work-for-her. Unless you want to take that one out for a spin now?" my dad said, looking at my mom.

"Let's go get pancakes!" my mom said, surrendering and taking my hand.

We used the time at breakfast to talk about normal things, all of us feeling saturated with more questions than answers about 'the property' as we had all started referring to it. The temporary embargo on the 'property' talk lifted when we finished eating. My mom always did better when she had a good and solid pro/con list on big decisions, so we opted to start one together. I grabbed one of the small notebooks I always kept in my purse, for such a time as this, and we huddled around the café table and got to work.

Several pieces of notebook paper, cups of coffee and contented bellies later, we had quite the list going. I closed the notebook and set the pen down. "I cannot think anymore, my brain stem has detached itself from my body and is making a run for it." I said, dramatically putting my head down on my notepad.

"We also probably need to return this table to its rightful owners," Mom said, looking around the café. It looked like the breakfast crowd was gone and the lunch rush was getting ready to start up. "Let's get out of here and get some fresh air." She picked up her purse and stood, groaning as she did. "I think my body has molded itself to that chair."

My dad got up slowly, his body also revolting against the new movement. I kept my head down hoping that if I just stayed still, they would forget I was there and allow me to nap in the current, but rather uncomfortable, position I seemed to be folded in. My mom grabbed the notebook out from under my face, leaving me no choice but to sit up or end up with my face smashed on the table. Gross. "Traitor," I said, handing her the pen and forcing myself to stand. "Lead me to this outside and fresh air you speak of." I made ample use of air quotes to accentuate the foreignness of those words.

We ended up walking around the little shops that were near the café, making small talk and buying absolutely zero things. By the time we piled back into the car, our minds were a little less worse-for-wear and our energy levels were restored. This was a very good thing since the second we got in the car each one of our phones started dinging and ringing and doing what any good phone would do.

"And so it begins," my dad said, sending his brother Simon to voicemail. I tossed my phone across the backseat and rested my head against the headrest. I had a feeling this was not something we were going to be able to avoid talking about again for the rest of the day.

"Let's get home and then you can call your brothers back," my mom said to my dad after she finished listening to a voicemail. "I'll need to call my parents too. I missed a call while we were shopping, and it sounds like they told my sister. She has questions. They also wanted to check in and see if there were any new developments."

Since the rest of the family was plying both my parents for details, I knew that the text message dings that were happening on my phone were either Emily or Holly. If it wasn't them, it was work, and it was my day off so they could just... not. "I think we're also going to have to talk to Grandma again at some point," I pointed out, closing my eyes and taking a deep breath.

Looking over her shoulder, my mom asked, "How would you feel if we brought everyone back over for dinner? It's not ideal, but at least we can kill multiple birds with one stone..." she trailed off, looking out her window. That let me know she wasn't really excited about her plan either, even if it was the path of least resistance.

"I'd prefer to not kill any birds, especially with stones. That just sounds cruel. As for dinner, I'd really rather not, but I do have to head back home the day after tomorrow, so it's not like we have a lot of time to figure some things out. I do vote we do something simple like order pizza, or make other people bring us food since we're hosting again. And by 'we're' I mean you. Also... ice cream. They should bring ice cream."

"Maybe Mom and I should go to Grandma's place for dinner instead?" My dad said, looking at my mom for agreement. I sat up and made eye contact with him in the rearview mirror. "I'm just thinking that there's more to discuss between us before we get everyone else involved."

"By everyone else, I'm assuming you're talking about my family?" I could hear the tightness in her voice and couldn't help feeling bad. We both knew that first and foremost the decision my grandmother made was between her, and her boys, and their wives. But my mom didn't think like they did, and I could imagine that she'd feel less outnumbered if she could have her parents with her, even if they said nothing. I know I always felt better making big decisions when I could work it out with my parents first, even if they just acted as sounding boards. My dad, to his credit, had the decency to look pained at what he knew he was asking.

Mom sighed. "You're right. It would be better to have the discussion without all the extra opinions. Paige, are you comfortable with that?"

"No, but also yes. I mean there is no point in me worrying about what role I'm going to play in all of this if something changes and Grandma doesn't end up keeping the property... although I have to admit I think the chances of that happening are very slim. I do also agree that Grandma not having everyone throwing their opinions at her might help get more accomplished in the conversation that needs to happen. So maybe you two go have dinner with her tonight, and we meet up with Holly, Grandma, and Grandpa tomorrow once we know more. In the meantime, I can do some thinking and some praying to get my own ducks in a row."

It took all of two seconds after my parents left for me to realize that by them having dinner with Grandma, I got the entire night to myself. Doing a little dance of joy, I headed up to my parents' bathroom and their giant soaker tub. Immediately turned the water on, waiting until it got to just below scalding, then let it start to fill. I added some lavender bath salts and then headed to my room to grab my pajamas and a book. I fully planned on soaking in that water until either it became too cold to stay in, or I turned into a wrinkly old prune, whichever came first.

Turned out the prune won, and I finally pulled myself out of the water, wrapping my long dark hair in a towel and applying all the creams and lotions that made me feel like I was at a fancy day spa before slipping into my cozy pjs. As I headed downstairs to rustle up some dinner, I dialed Emily's number.

"I have questions..." Emily said after the first ring.

"Hello dear, how was your day?" I said in response. I loved a good and proper greeting. Manners matter.

"Hello. I have questions that we're going to need answers to... first, and most importantly, you're going to need to figure out what your options are when it comes to work. Can you take a personal leave for a few months without having to quit or lose your benefits? Once we know that, I think we need to figure out what to do with the apartment and your half of the rent... no offense. I also think that she needs to give you a scope of responsibilities and expectation in writing so you can figure out if you are comfortable with all of them... also, I did a little research and there are some classes that I think you could take at the local community college for the hospitality industry and business management and I think she should pay for those."

"If I do this, you mean..." I said, trying to put a break in the laundry list of to-dos since I had written precisely zero of them down.

"If you decide to do this, yes..."

"And you?"

"Truthfully? I think it's ridiculous and crazy. I also think it sounds like it could be fun. So obviously my job comes first, and I'm hashtag Team Paige all the way, so I will follow your lead, but you are all my family too, so..."

"She had a dream..."

"I feel like this could be a trick..."

"No, she really did have a dream... your mom was in it. My grandma said she was the deciding factor." There was silence on the other end of the phone. "Em? If we do this, I feel like your mom needs to be a part of it too... I mean even more than bossing us around and making my grandma buy a bed and breakfast. She's part of this family too..."

"I think she'd like that." Emily said, her voice cracking just enough to let me know that the weight of what I said was not lost on her either.

"So... if we do this..."

"Yes?"

"The first thing I should admit is that I wrote none of this down..." I said, sheepishly

"I already sent you everything in an email, including the link to the courses I think could be helpful, but feel free to poke around and see if there is anything else interesting."

"Like underwater basket weaving?"

"How would that help you renovate a bed and breakfast?"

"Guests need activities, obviously. Come on, you're the events guru!"

"Do you have somewhere where your guests could be underwater?" Emily said. I could hear the eye roll in her voice.

"I have no idea... but don't you think we should be prepared, just in case?"

"Not really."

"Party-pooper.

"That's why you invited me."

"Well played, Em. Well played."

"Thank you. Do your homework and call me tomorrow, I'm off all day."

"Ugh, I graduated so I wouldn't have homework anymore!" I sighed.

"Don't lie. You didn't even do your homework when you were in school."

"You're just jealous because I was able to get A's in all my classes without trying."

"Without attending, you mean."

"It's a gift, it really is."

"Well, this homework counts as all your credit, smarty pants. And stop sticking your tongue out at me," Em scolded.

I put my tongue back in my mouth, even though I knew she couldn't see me. "Fine, but I'm hanging up now. Dinner is calling my name."

"Call me tomorrow."

"I'll think about it."

"You will."

"I will. Have a good night."

"Bye Paige."

"Bye Em."

CHAPTER THREE

Is That your Final Answer?

"I'm going to get the bed and breakfast started for Grandma."

It was a couple of weeks after Halloween, and I had met my parents for dinner down the street from my mom's work. I tried to wait until neither of my parents had anything in their mouths as a safety precaution before making my announcement. I didn't want them to choke on anything. I wasn't sure if I remembered how to perform the Heimlich maneuver and I was absolutely sure that it would not help anything if immediately following my announcement one or both of my parents needed to seek emergency medical attention.

"You are? What about your job? And your apartment? How is that all going to work?" My mom started down the path of all the questions that had plagued me for the past few weeks. I don't know whether or not she was really hoping for me to turn down the offer, or if she was just processing her emotions externally. Either way, I knew that once she was finished, she'd be ready to hear the answers to all the questions she was rapid firing in my direction.

My dad, on the other hand sat quietly, attempting to mask the concern he also felt in the decision I'd just announced. Dad was always the one who externally showed support for whatever his daughters told him, but worried internally. Mom was the exact opposite. Both always came around once the initial reaction phase was over and we could have a conversation to walk through the steps that led to the decision. It was a process I sometimes wished we could speed up or avoid, but knowing in the end my parents meant it when they gave me their support or were proud of me and trusted my decisions made the steps well worth it.

My mom's line of rhetorical questioning finally ran out of steam, and she looked at me with worry lines creasing her forehead. I took another bite of my spaghetti. "So, how did you decide you want to do this?" My dad asked his question calmly, taking another bite of his dinner when he was done.

"Well, I've been struggling with just going through the motions at my job for a while now, which is no secret to either of you. I've only really been staying because I feel like I owe Jennifer for all the time and belief she's invested in me, and because I haven't found another job that would pay my bills and still allow me to prioritize the more important things in my life. This opportunity easily solves the latter, and I had a long conversation with Jennifer. She actually thinks it's a great step. She can't keep me employed during the time I would be setting up the B and B, but she said she will definitely hire me back, if I decide that is what I want to do once I finish with the opening. She actually mentioned how the experience could open more opportunities for me with the part of her company that deals with expansion, and restaurant design.

"So really, no matter how all of this turns out, barring a major disaster, this kind of lends itself to getting me unstuck in my regular life too." I paused to stab a piece of my meatball. "And obviously I've spent a lot of time praying about it and talking to God, and I just know in my know-er that I'm supposed to do this with Grandma. And with all of you. This really is a once-in-a-lifetime opportunity, and I am not willing to put anything else before this time with the family. As for the apartment, for now the plan is to keep paying my half of the rent in the short term, and then Em and I will revisit when our lease is up at the end of January... that is if you are willing to let me come live with you for a little while..."

"Of course, you're always welcome with us, you know that" my mom said, looking contemplative. "I would love having more time with you, and it would bring you home for the holidays for the first time in who knows how many years, which is nothing but a blessing..."

"But?" I asked, stabbing another meatball piece.

"But... I don't know... it feels risky. Which doesn't make it bad of course. It's just outside of my comfort zone. It's going to be a crazy amount of work, and Grandma can be a tough boss. I don't want anything to ruin your relationship either." My mom stabbed a bite of her meatball and continued to think, the worry lines starting to relax on her face. The truth was, aside from the actual work and business part of things, it really was a very stable way of exiting one career and entering another. My grandmother, while fronting quite a bit of money into buying the property and the expectations of renovating it, had not wrapped her entire life savings into this endeavor, which meant my financial situation was just as stable going into this experiment as it was in its current form. My parents had lived with me for the first twenty-three years of my life, so it wasn't like they didn't know what to expect from me as a roommate.

"I will, of course, help contribute to the bills and food and do my own laundry and whatever you need around the house..." I started and then trailed off as both my parents rolled their eyes and shook their heads.

"We're not worried about any of that," my dad said. "We just want to make sure you've thought this all the way through. Which it sounds like you have."

I reached both my hands across the table and took one of each of their extended hands. "I promise you that I have put more prayer, thought, and effort into this decision than I have in almost any other I've ever made. I know on the surface it sounds crazy; I still think so too sometimes. But I really do think it's going to be great for me, and great for the family. I think it's going to be frustrating and hard and stretch me and make me uncomfortable... and I think it's going to be fun. I want to do this. I want to go on this adventure with Grandma, and with all of you. Emily is also on board, as much as her workload will allow. She agrees it's time for a bit of a shakeup. Besides, can you look me in the eye and honestly tell me you haven't started daydreaming about decorating all those rooms? No, you cannot," I answered for them.

"So... what happens next?" My dad asked. He didn't seem to have any further questions, at the moment, about my decision and was ready to talk about the next step.

"Truthfully, I'm not really sure. I've already called Grandma and told her I'm in. And I officially gave my notice to Jennifer, so I'm going to finish this week out at work, then get everything I need to relocate back home. If you're good with it, I'll be moving in next weekend. Then bright and early next Monday, I'll be picking up my new boss and we'll head to her property to talk about the next steps. You are both invited to go with, if you want, but that will depend on your job schedules. I haven't yet signed up for any of the courses Emily found because they don't start until the new year, but I did find a few online programs that I think could be beneficial, so Grandma has instructed me to enroll in those."

No one said anything for a few minutes. Instead, we all just nibbled on our food and let everything sink in. I knew my father would end up coming with us to the property because he could not resist an adventure. He also worked from home, which made his schedule a bit more flexible when he wasn't traveling for work. My mom was the one who held a more traditional Monday through Friday, nine to five job, so she probably wasn't going to be able to join. I made a mental note to find time that would work for her to make sure she got the tour and game plan too.

"Nancy? Are you sure we want to be taking on boarders at our age?" My dad said, smiling wickedly in my direction.

"At our age? Speak for yourself!" My mom feigned being insulted at the insinuation she was anything close to 'old.' "I think a boarder could be great. She'd eat vegetables without complaint."

"It's true, I would." I said, agreeing with my mom. "I'm pretty great that way."

"I will look at my calendar tomorrow when I get to work, but I probably won't be able to go with you guys on Monday. But if I'm supposed to be figuring out how to decorate this place, you better take some really great pictures," my mom said. And that was it. The decision had been made. We had talked about it, and all of a sudden, we were all on the same page. The Donovan family was renovating a bed and breakfast.

"You do know we're going to have to get Uncle Simon and Uncle Derrick on board at some point, right? I don't know how that will go," my dad said, sitting back contentedly.

"And Holly," I added, throwing my napkin onto the table. I knew she was still very frustrated with how presumptuous she thought Grandma had been toward my life and career. I loved that she was protective of me. I also knew that when the time came, she'd hop on board this crazy train right alongside me. We had each other's backs when it mattered most. No questions asked.

"I feel like this evening has already been plenty eventful. How about we cross those bridges later?" My mom suggested. My dad and I agreed whole-heartedly, and the rest of the evening was spent talking about how things were going at both my parents' jobs. It sounded like the bed and breakfast was going to be a good change for more than just me. Everyone needed a bit of an escape from their routine. None of us knew precisely how much of an escape from our routine we were in store for.

The week went by in a flash, and before I knew it, I was unpacking boxes and suitcases into my new room at my parents' house. It took most of the weekend to get myself settled and come up with the semblance of a game plan for my first official day on the job. Monday morning, my dad and I were at my grandma's place promptly at nine. We had left the house early and stopped to grab a light breakfast and some coffee. I wanted to make sure that I had everything I might need for the next few hours, so I had made myself a little kit containing all the supplies I could think of including—but not limited to—notepads for each of us with different colored pens so we could easily refer to our notes and compare. A couple of measuring tapes, portable charging pods to ensure we didn't run out of camera juice before capturing all the video and photos we might need, a couple of small but annoyingly bright flashlights, and some blue painters tape. Why I had the tape, I wasn't sure, but I had it, nonetheless. I wasn't sure exactly what to expect at the property, but I knew that it was always best to be prepared.

My dad ran upstairs to my grandma's apartment while I waited in the car in the loading zone. I asked him to make sure that she was wearing something that could get dirty as well as comfortable walking shoes, just in case. Grandma Jane had reassured me the night before that the property was in good shape overall, but I was determined to be overly cautious; she may have become my boss as of seventeen minutes ago, but first and foremost she was my grandmother. As I sat in the car waiting for the two of them to return, an excited but nervous energy started to hum inside me. For as long as I can remember, my grandmother held this place in my heart that exemplified power and professionalism. She had always been a leader in her industry, and as a woman growing up when she did, that was no small feat. Each of my grandparents meant the world to me in different ways, and they all filled different roles and paths of guidance in my heart.

Grandma Rose was the heart of our family. She taught me the importance of serving others well and loving them even better. She was the one who took care of me when I was sick, sacrificed her time and her money to help contribute to whatever we needed—the amount of fundraising wrapping paper and ceramic mugs that woman owned to help me participate in choir could fill an entire section of a store. She was also the one who hosted almost all of our holidays, taught me to cook, and reminded me that love is something that is a physical act, not just a verbal platitude. She also had this sneaky, adventurous, and rebellious side that spoke to the same traits in me. Out of all my grandparents, Grandma Rose is who I resemble most.

Grandpa Frank was a hard worker and a risk taker. He learned most of what he knew from the school of life, having grown up during The Great Depression. He believed hard work and smart decisions would get you far. Being a kind and decent human being would help get you the rest of the way. My grandfather is a really good man. And his laugh lights up a room, and anyone lucky enough to hear it.

My Grandpa Jimmy passed away when I was very young. I don't have any direct memories of him, but he lives on through the stories my family has passed on to me. I got my love of music and the arts from him, and those qualities were nurtured by my Aunt Lynn and Uncle Robert, who helped grow my love of books and stories, and took me to concerts, musicals, and plays as I grew up.

When I thought of my Grandma Jane, I always thought of the amazing example she set being a working woman with a very successful career and raising three boys. She retired when I was in junior high, and I remember going to her retirement party and seeing all the people who came to celebrate her because she had touched their lives through her work. She was so respected and loved and the presence she held in that room was something I can still picture vividly so many years later. As a woman who prided herself on being a firm but fair boss, with high expectations for those who worked for her, I found myself unsure of being able to live up to those sentiments that I admired in her so much. I wanted to, or rather was determined to, make her proud, and I knew she was counting on me.

Dad and Grandma finally got to the car, and climbed in. We said our hellos and then Jane became all business. "So, tell me what the plan is, Paige," she instructed, all traces of the grandma voice I was used to having been replaced with boss-lady vibrato. I was sitting in the back seat directly behind her, so I quickly unbuckled and scooted across to the other side, and then buckled myself back in before my father made it out of the driveway. I wanted her to be able to see me as I spoke if she wanted to.

"I believe the most important thing to do today is to take a thorough look at the property and start lists of what needs to be done. I expect that this effort will take us half of the day onsite, and the remainder of the day to compile the list. I have everything we need in order to conduct our own inspection of the property, as well as a list of inventory, measurements of the rooms, or anything else we may need measurements for. I would also like to talk to the current owner and gather information from her regarding staff, guests, and contractors who have, or have done, business with the bed and breakfast in the past. I have started some initial research based on what I could find on the internet, but I'd like to get a feel of the state of the business directly from her.

"Once we are finished at the property, I have made us reservations for lunch where we can sit and compare notes. I'll then spend tomorrow compiling and organizing the items we identify into a project plan, with timeline and budgetary considerations, as well as contacts for the quoting process to determine who we will be requesting bids from for the actual work. I am hoping to have that completed and to you by the end of this week." I said, taking a breath. Grandma Jane didn't say anything, she simply nodded her head in agreement. I paused a little longer to see if she had any questions or anything she wanted to say, but she seemed content to let me continue.

"I have already spoken with both Mr. Jameson the realtor, and Mrs. Morey, the current proprietor. They will be meeting us there at 9:30. I believe we will be able to consolidate the project timeline by ensuring all parties are present and prepared to share information and task lists." My phone chimed and I paused to check the text message. It was from Mr. Jameson letting me know he had arrived a little early and would be in his car. I quickly sent a response thanking him and letting him know we were about ten minutes away and we would see him shortly. I also mentioned that Mrs. Morey would be meeting with us.

I filled my grandma and my dad in on what Mr. Jameson said, to which my dad made eye contact with me through his rearview mirror and winked, letting me know he thought I was doing a fine job. "I also spoke with Ben this weekend, and he is going to come with me when I have the trades bid on the projects, to make sure he agrees with what is being said and quoted. He has some contacts on foremen through his architecture firm who he has recommended. He has also offered to help with sketches and blueprints if we need them."

"He did? I don't want him to feel like he has to do us any favors... we can pay him, and his firm for their services if we think they are necessary," my grandmother added.

"I agree and have mentioned that to him, but he wasn't sure we'd need that level of involvement from them, so for now he would like to exercise his position as part of this family to contribute to the new family business. I also may have mentioned that I could teach Holly how to make his favorite pasta dish..." I said, smiling at my dad.

"Bribery and little sister mischief. I like it," my dad said laughing.

My grandmother turned around and smiled. "We have a very busy day ahead of us, but I think your plan will serve us well." I slowly let out the breath I hadn't realized I was holding. I set my head back on the headrest and looked out the window for a minute. Now that the official business was concluded, my boss quickly disappeared and my grandmother returned in her place, asking my dad about his work and if he'd spoken to his brothers at all over the weekend. I tuned out most of the conversation, content to organize my thoughts and mentally revisit my plan to make sure I was prepared when we arrived.

My mom was sad that she couldn't come with us to see the property, but she had some meetings that she couldn't reschedule. I promised her before she left for work that morning that I would make sure to capture some video and all the pictures.

Gazing out the window, I noticed that the area we were in was absolutely beautiful. Rolling green hills smattered with trees that were showing off their autumn plumage as far as the eye could see. I was hopeful that the view from the bed and breakfast would be equally as beautiful. There was an adorable vintage style main street only a few blocks away from the bed and breakfast, making it a great spot for visitors as well. I was hoping the bed and breakfast had a bit of personality to it already, but not so much that we wouldn't be able to somehow infuse ourselves into it. I had some ideas that I hadn't shared with anyone yet, but that I thought could make things very special for our family.

I saw the property before we got to it. As we turned the final corner, I saw a tall, majestic looking Victorian complete with gingerbread siding, bay windows, and spires. It even had an adorable weathervane at the top of the main peak, although we were still too far away for me to make out what it was. The structure sat alone on a hill, and it looked to be surrounded by multiple gardens. I knew it was the place before my grandmother had a chance to say anything. She pointed and said, "There! Look at it!" and in those four words, I heard the excitement in her voice and understood exactly why she had fallen in love with it.

As we pulled up the long and winding driveway, an image of Laurie sitting next to me popped into my mind. She smiled at me with a look that said "See what all the fuss is about? Doesn't it already feel like home?" and I couldn't help but smile back at the vision because she was completely right. It already felt like a part of the family; and family is what home is all about.

CHAPTER FOUR

What's in a Name?

The main house was spectacular. The long and winding driveway gave way to a small gravel parking lot off to the side, near what would be called the guest house if this was still the single-family mansion it was originally created to be. I suspected this was the structure that my grandmother meant I could move into when it was ready if I wanted to, and I made a mental note to come back to explore that structure later. Today was all about the main building and the grounds.

From the front, the foundation was built up, allowing for five or six steps to get to the porch. The porch itself was huge and looked like it wrapped all the way around the house. There also seemed to be three different areas that were built out of the house creating depth and the feeling of texture. I wasn't sure what was in those three rooms, but I made a mental note that they could probably become large suites if they were not already. I paused before climbing out of the car to grab the notepads and pens and pass them to my dad and grandma since ideas were already flying through my mind.

Once out of the car, I paused and continued to take in the main structure. It had a dark roof and was painted a light green color with both tan and white trim. It looked like it was going to need a fresh coat of paint. There were windows everywhere, covered with lace curtains. The front door of the house was landscaped beautifully but hadn't been tended to in a while. On either side of the main house were gardens. My grandmother and dad were met by Mr. Jameson who was ready to take them inside. I wasn't quite done taking in the outside or jotting down quick notes to help me remember my first impressions, so I let them know I'd be right behind them.

As I stood there, my mind filled with all sorts of different ideas regarding the potential of the place. I started to feel incredibly overwhelmed. Who was I to think I could take on a project like this? Whispered a sarcastic voice in my mind. I'd been around long enough to know that whispers like that could get a girl in trouble pretty quickly if she listened to them, so I closed my eyes and sent a quick prayer heavenward to help keep me focused on the present. If God believed I could do this, then He would also make sure he wasn't wrong in that belief. "Give me a sign, Lord," I whispered, making an active attempt to slow and deepen my breathing. Right then I saw two hummingbirds dancing in the air just above one of the side garden gates. They hovered for a moment; heads turned in my direction as if to say 'Come take a look! We have something we want you to see!' I headed in that direction and when I got closer, they flew further into the garden, never out of sight, simply out of reach. When I looked, I realized there weren't just two hummingbirds, but somewhere between six and ten. I'd never seen so many in one place in my life. I couldn't help but let a laugh of surprise escape my lips. "Thank you, Lord." I said, smiling up at the heavens and then watching the hummingbirds as they danced and played in their garden.

"They're amazing, aren't they?"

I turned quickly, startled by the voice behind me. An attractive looking woman, probably in her late sixties, was standing at the edge of the garden. "I've never seen so many at one time before," she said, "But this garden is my favorite because of the birds and butterflies that love to visit."

"You must be Mrs. Morey!" I said, smiling back and offering my hand.

"Please, call me Sara. You must be Paige, Jane's granddaughter."

"I am. It's a pleasure to meet you. I'm sorry that I wasn't inside with my grandmother and dad, I just needed a moment to finish taking in the beauty of the place and then the hummingbirds caught my attention..."

"There is no need to apologize. Walking through these gardens has always been one of my favorite pastimes. We were just getting ready to take a tour of the inside of the bed and breakfast, and I just wanted to see if you would like to join us."

I nodded and turned my full attention to Sara as we started to head back to the front door. "That would be great, thank you so much for coming and getting me." As we entered the front door, I was greeted by the front desk area with a small sitting area that doubled as a library off to the side. My grandma and dad were sitting in a couple of chairs across from Mr. Jameson.

"There you are. We were wondering where you'd gone," my grandma said as I walked over to her.

"Sorry, I was just trying to take it all in and I got a little distracted by one of the side gardens."

"Well, if you are all ready, shall we begin the tour?" Mr. Jameson said, standing and gesturing toward the front desk. I helped my grandma stand and she tucked her hand in my father's arm so that he could assist her in getting around. I headed to the front desk area where I made sure my pen and notepad were poised and at the ready.

The tour of the house lasted a couple of hours. Overall, it was absolutely gorgeous, and had great bones. There was definitely some updating and cosmetic work that was going to need to be done so that we didn't feel like we were living in the mid-nineteenth century, but there were also several areas that had already been redone and outfitted with more modern touches.

The kitchen was one such location, which was a huge relief. I knew kitchens could be incredibly expensive to overhaul, especially when having to bring them up to code. I let out an audible breath when I saw the new, state-of-the-art appliances. The large ten-burner stove complete with built in griddle and pot filler would be a chef's dream. The room also boasted oversized windows, and two French doors that led out onto the wraparound porch and let in tons of light. It was simply decorated, but quite pretty.

I jotted down a few notes in each of the rooms we visited and took pictures and video while my father took down measurements. I already had several ideas, some of which would involve the moving or complete removal of walls to maximize room space as well as allow for unique views from most of the would-be guest rooms.

The outdoor space was full of life, some of which seemed to be wild and on a rampant growth spurt. I took down a lot of notes as we wandered the divided gardens, as I knew landscaping could also become an area where money disappeared quickly. As we moved through each of the garden areas, and then started down a winding path that would also need some repair, I noticed that there wasn't any space reserved for outdoor entertainment. I wrote this down as a must, already thinking about summer evening dining events, tea parties, bridal and baby showers, or even an occasional small wedding that could take place if the gardens were designed in a way to allow for it. I also circled that particular note to make sure I got Emily a copy of the images, so she could help with ensuring the design was one that was versatile but not sterile for the variety of events that could be held there.

The path itself led us down to an area with some beautiful trees and a small lawn, private enough for a quiet afternoon of reading, or a small picnic. Beyond that there was a small swimming pool and spa. The pool area definitely had not had any attention in recent years, but it did have potential. My grandmother had decided to stay up on the porch instead of wandering the gardens with us because of the uneven surfaces, so I made sure to take pictures and videos so that she could get a really good feel for the grounds.

After the tour, we spent some time back in the sitting area of the main house talking with Mr. Jameson and Mrs. Morey. It was great to get a feel for the history of the place, as well as the staff that had worked there. I took a ton of notes and Sara promised to send me all the information she had digitally for my use. She pulled out the reservation book—the fact that this was a literal physical book was not lost on me—to see who already had reservations in the first of the year. Thankfully, prior to putting the property on the market, Sara had already decided to close the bed and breakfast for November and December so that she could spend the holidays with her family back east. It wasn't until later that she decided that she really wanted to stay closer to her family, and the idea of putting the bed and breakfast on the market was born.

My grandma, dad, and I left the property close to 2:00, and by that time we were starving. We were right on schedule to keep our lunch reservation and discuss everything we'd just seen and learned. I also wanted to start working on the name for the place, since "Bed and Breakfast" was entirely too long to keep saying, "B&B" sounded like we were trying too hard to be cool, and "the property" makes it sound like we're talking about a dirt lot. I also wanted to run an idea by my grandma because after taking in the property, I thought it felt more like an inn than a bed and breakfast, and I was hoping she'd agree with the vision.

Once we were seated at a small café that has delicious sandwiches and the best potato salad you've ever had in your life, I pulled out all our notebooks and we got down to work. We quickly agreed that all the guest rooms needed to be renovated, bathrooms updated and modernized, then painted and redecorated.

There was a lot of work that would need to be done on the update and maintenance front. Once that portion was complete, the redecorating could begin. That was the part my mom was going to really look forward to once she got to see all the pictures we took, as well as the renderings I was going to have Ben help with. The final piece I wanted to make sure we addressed was updating the technology side of the business. Or should I say, create technology for the business. Mrs. Morey was a self-proclaimed computer illiterate, which is why she still used the paper date book and desk calendar to maintain her reservation records. Guests would call and have to get someone live on the phone in order to make a reservation, and if they had any sort of special instructions, that was marked in the calendar by the fancy use of... wait for it... a post-it note.

Creating a website and obtaining reservation software as well as adding an inventory system that could help track expenses, aid in budgeting and forecasting needs would be incredibly valuable. I added a note to determine what was being used for taxes, payroll, and all the accounting things that would go with running a business. I had some knowledge in the technology space, but the truth was it was probably going to be more prudent to get some help.

My grandmother seemed to be okay with everything I was discussing so far, but I once again realized that there was a lot of work that needed to be done and that overwhelmed feeling started to reappear. I was starting to realize that it wasn't just the renovation part that was going to take significant time and attention, but also the execution of the business side of things. It was an entirely parallel project.

I decided that the next day was going to be spent organizing myself and creating a timeline. I needed to get my hands around the entire picture. I kept coming up with lists of things that I needed to make sure were accounted for.

As the sandwiches were put in front of us, I realized I was making a list of all the lists I'd need. My grandmother cleared her throat and indicated toward my sandwich with her eyes letting me know I should eat. "Sorry, I just... there is so much to do. I don't want to forget anything." I put my pen down and closed my notebook.

"How about we all take a little break from the planning, and we just enjoy our lunch?" my dad said, knowing that if my head kept spinning the way it was, there was a reasonable chance it would spin itself right off my neck. I let out a slow breath and nodded. He was right. It was time to let my brain cells digest all they had seen and heard over the last several hours.

We enjoyed the rest of our lunch, talking about anything but the giant bed and breakfast shaped elephant in the room. My grandma had plans later that week with some of her friends for dinner and a local production of My Fair Lady, so she told us all the details. I had never seen the stage production, but I did love the story. I pictured the scene where Henry Higgins first lays eyes on Eliza Doolittle, the cockney flower woman... Speaking of flowers...

"Grandma, would you mind if I took Grandpa Frank to look at the gardens before I find a landscape architect? I want to get a feel for what could grow well and maybe even see if we could have a small vegetable garden that could be used for our menus."

"I think that's a lovely idea. Frank loves projects like this." There was a gleam in her eye that I hadn't seen in a while. I could tell that she was already starting to see the seeds of her plan taking root, and she was happy.

"So, what about me? How can I help?" my dad asked, drawing my attention away from my grandma and her meddling ways.

"Well, I was hoping that you might want to run to the store with me later today to get supplies so that I can get organized. When we're ready, I'd love it if you could help me interview people for the trades we'll need. Finally, I was hoping that while I spend tomorrow getting myself set up, you two could go and get whatever we need done at the bank in order to give me access to money. I will leave that up to you, Grandma, on how you want that to work, but I think it would be smart if we both could pay the bills." I knew my dad was starting to get excited too, now that he'd seen the property. My grandma wasn't being dramatic when she said this was going to be a family affair. I was going to need everyone to do their part if there was even the smallest chance we'd be ready for the first of the year.

I sent a quick text to Emily asking if she could let me know a day the following week that she might be able to spend with me. I needed to get her the rundown of what was going on, what we needed, and where she thought she could be most helpful. I also wanted her to see the property so she could get a feel for the place. Ugh. The place. I really needed to get a name sorted out.

"Who you talking to?" my dad asked, always wondering if he was missing out on something good.

"Emily. I was hoping she could come out for a day or two next week so I could get her up to speed. Nosy pants." I speared a piece of potato salad with my fork and popped it into my mouth. Delicious.

"What did she say?" my dad asked as my phone buzzed. I gave him a look stern enough to make him turn sheepish. "Sorry, I like to be in the know."

"She said 'thumbs up'" I said, shaking my head and smiling. "Is there anything I should tell her from you, or does this conversation suffice for now?"

"It suffices... for now." My dad answered, taking his own bite of potato salad and looking proud of himself.

We finished our lunch and headed back to grandma's house. As we walked her to her apartment, she asked that we meet again before the weekend to get an update on where I was. I told her I'd come and spend some time with her on Wednesday and then again on Friday. I asked if she had access to email, to which she said yes, but that she had never had reason to access it before, so she didn't have an actual account. I added that to my list of things that we'd need to take care of on Wednesday when we met. I knew it would be a lot easier for her to keep tabs on things if I could copy her on emails and communications, as well as send summaries of accomplishments and to-dos. I also wanted to make sure she had veto power since she was the owner, and my boss.

"I can use the computer in the library for now," she said as I mentioned we might want to think about getting her a laptop. "You can reach me by phone most of the time if I'm not with you, otherwise I will plan on checking email each day for now. If after that we decide a laptop is still needed, we can cross that bridge at that time. I have no other use for the thing."

"I can teach you many other uses, Grandma. Writing, games, finding movies and shows. Even how to search for ideas on things you might want for the inn."

"The inn?" she asked, surprised.

Whoops. I hadn't mentioned that out loud yet. "Sorry, I mean the bed and breakfast."

"I don't think you did. You think it should be an inn?" my grandma asked, sitting down on her couch. My dad and I hadn't planned on staying long, but I sat on the arm of her chair anyways, figuring now was as good a time as any.

"I mean... I know people like the concept of a bed and breakfast, and that is what you had pictured... but to me it felt more like a cozy little inn. Small and personalized... cozy."

"I like the idea of an inn," my dad said. "It feels very Gilmore Girls-ey."

My grandmother just looked at me, and then at my father. "I have no idea what you're talking about, son, but I like the idea of an inn..." my grandmother trailed off, thoughtfully.

"Gilmore Girls was a show... you know what? It doesn't matter. Just know it was a compliment," Dad said smiling.

Grandma Jane was not a huge television fan. She watched the news and a couple of other shows, but mostly she couldn't be bothered. Books she could do for hours on end, but she just never found the same love for television or movies. Grandma shrugged at Dad's comment. Knowing it was meant to be a compliment seemed to suffice.

I stood up, sensing that the events of the day had worn Grandma down and she needed some time to rest and decompress. I gave her a quick kiss on the cheek, and my dad followed suit. Dad asked, "Is there anything else you need before we leave?"

"I'm going to need a trip to the store later this week. I'm almost out of milk. Other than that, I'm all set," she said, slipping out of her shoes and into her slippers.

"I'll call you tomorrow. Maybe when you're done with Paige on Wednesday we can run to the store. I have some clients tomorrow, so I won't be able to do it then."

"That's fine. Wednesday will work perfectly," she waved to us as she started to lie down on the sofa and pull a blanket over herself.

"We'll talk tomorrow too, Grandma. Love you!" I said as I opened the door and started out. Grandma Jane propped herself up a little, calling to me. I turned back and paused in the doorway so I could hear her.

"Paige, before you go, I have one more question I'm going to need you to think about."

"What's that?" I asked.

"Think about what you'd like to call the place. I believe it is in need of a new name."

The thing was, I already knew. As soon as my grandmother posed the question out loud, I realized I had known since the moment I was standing in the garden thinking about Laurie and hearing from the Lord.

"Hummingbird Hollow. I think we should call it Hummingbird Hollow."

CHAPTER FIVE

Holy Crap!

Two weeks later, I was sitting in my car at the top of my parent's street, cell phone on the dash, my poor Phoebe all covered with files and papers, her cup holders filled with now-empty coffee cups and a Hydro flask laying precariously between the cups and the passenger seat. I should not have been surprised at how much of my business was conducted sitting in my car at the top of the street, but I was. Most days I would head either to a coffee shop or the library to get work done, but when I just needed a few minutes to make some phone calls, driving all the way to those places felt wasteful so I just ended up at the top of the street.

It was the Monday before Thanksgiving and at that moment I could not for the life of me remember why I made the decision to leave my job and take on a project the size of the inn. I spent the weekend working at the main house because the plumber wanted to get through as much work as he could before the holiday, and the electrician apparently felt the same way. The electrician was in fact the reason I found myself sitting at the top of the street adding 'car wash' to the day's tasks. He wanted to push back the rest of the work until late the following week because one of his guys had decided to take a few extra days off with his family. He could sense the stress in my voice as I hesitated to the agreement, but he reassured me that he would still be able to meet his deadline without issue.

I had become a very quick study over the past few weeks but still relied heavily on my brother-in-law and his advice to get me through conversations with the trades. He was overseeing most of the work on our behalf because he knew it would save Grandma Jane a chunk of change if I didn't have to hire a foreman. I was in awe of what he had helped accomplish and found myself both humbled and extra grateful to him this year. The main thing he taught me is that timeline was everything. There was a rhythm to the order in which things needed to get done, and if even one of the trades slipped, the entire timeline could end up getting pushed back. That part was zero fun.

The following week I was supposed to pick out paint and the furnishings for the guest rooms. My mom and aunt were going to go with me. I had an idea on how I wanted each room to be themed, but I wasn't one hundred percent set in my vision. The other part I was contending with was the fact that I wanted it to be a surprise for my family. I wasn't sure if I was being ridiculous since it was going to prove very difficult to have people help me decorate all while not allowing them to view the rooms in progress or how anything was being pulled together. I was pretty sure my mom and aunt were going to think I was crazy as I explained specifics on what we were in search of without giving any context of room or style.

I grabbed my iPad off of the seat next to me and I sent off an email to Ben to give him the update after the call with the electrician. I knew he'd check it later that afternoon and reach out if he had any questions or concerns. We were supposed to meet up at the inn that evening when he got off work so that he could have one of his contractor buddies do a quick inspection of the progress so far and let me know if there was anything else I needed to be following up on. When I finished sending off that email, I sent myself one reminding me to get thank you gifts to everyone who helped me in the project. They wouldn't be something large or expensive, just something small to show my appreciation for their efforts. I would never be able to pull off any of what we were doing without them, and I wanted them to know that.

Before I could meet Ben at the property, I had a date with my grandpa. I had a late afternoon meeting with the landscape architect we had selected, and I wanted to show the sketches to my grandpa before stamping a final approval on them. I'd had several conversations with Grandpa Frank and also my Uncle Robert about what the landscape architect, David, was recommending as well as what plants and vegetables they thought would enhance what we could use for the inn itself. David was working on making sure that the gardens looked beautiful but were not overly complicated to maintain. My grandpa and uncle thought the vegetable garden that the chef could use would be a great additional feature, but agreed with David in that the chef really should have final say in what would be beneficial to them once they were hired. In the meantime, my grandpa and uncle had given their thoughts on some staples that they felt any chef would appreciate having, like tomatoes and fresh herbs. I was very happy with the renderings David had created, putting all the ideas and suggestions together, and ensuring there was some room for additional growth once I'd had the opportunity to identify and hire the chef and get their input.

I checked the time and realized I had just enough before needing to be at my grandpa's house to swing by my favorite local joint and grab some iced coffee. I fired off a quick text to Emma, my high school best friend and the person who I had elected to be my confidant in the ideas I had for the guest rooms that I wanted to keep a surprise to everyone in the family. Emma had a great eye and knew my family because she'd grown up in it alongside me. I was hoping she could meet me later in the week for dinner so we could brainstorm. I then started up Phoebe and headed toward home to do a quick switcheroo of the things I had with me, to the things I needed. My car was great, but she was not a fully outfitted office and keeping organized was imperative at this stage of the game.

I headed into the house and ran up the stairs as quickly as possible, putting the files I had in my hand on the desk and grabbing the folders that contained the information from David. I kept my iPad and grabbed a different notebook and pen, which seemed to be my constant companions as of late.

"Hey! Where are you off to in such a hurry?" My dad called from wherever he had been hiding in the house upon my arrival. I headed back down the stairs, stopping midway on the landing to double check that I kept my purse and my keys with me during the useful item swap out.

"Grandma Rose and Grandpa Frank's house. But first, since I've been a very good girl today and done all my homework, I'm treating myself to an iced something-or-other-I-haven't-decided-yet coffee. Then I'm going to grab some lunch and hit up Target and the library before heading to Hummingbird Hollow to meet with David the landscape architect." I met my dad at the bottom of the stairs and paused long enough to be respectful and finish the conversation before heading out the door.

"Want company for lunch?"

"Always. As long as you promise you won't make me use big words or decide important things. I am planning on having a completely brain-free lunch." For the past week or so lunch had been an elective experience, often times looking like a meat stick and the emergency granola bars I kept in my backpack. If I had a few more minutes, it might look like a quick grab-and-go sandwich, a smoothie or anything else that could be consumed while moving either by foot or by car. Any time spent with my parents was either in the evening over dinner or at a meeting with my grandma, so having a sit-down lunch where I could spend time with my dad just being my dad sounded amazing. "You pick the place and send me a text and I will be there. I should be done at Grandma and Grandpa's by 1:00. I need to be at the Hollow by 3:30."

"Will do. See you in a bit," my dad said as I headed towards the door. "Drive safe and I love you," he finished as I got out the front door.

"Love you too!" I called over my shoulder, waving as he went to shut the door. I checked my cell phone once more as I started my car. I'd be pushing it, but if I hurried, I could still get to Grandpa after pausing at the caffeine-fueled promised land.

Grandpa Frank was ready for me when I arrived. I had called while I was in line at the drive thru to see if either he or my grandma wanted anything to drink. I knew they would both say no since they rarely drank anything caffeinated in the afternoons, but I always liked to ask just in case. Grandpa had been on his computer pulling up photos of the plants he thought would be good so that I could take them with me to the meeting. We sat out on the patio, and I showed him the plans.

"Do you have a water fountain or some sort of water feature anywhere? I was thinking that it could be really nice to have somewhere. Grandma and I always love to sit out here and listen to the fountain in the afternoon. It's very relaxing," my grandpa said, pointing over to the three-level fountain he had in the corner of his yard.

"I was thinking about getting something, and I mentioned it to David..." I sifted through the sketches until I found the right one. "We were thinking about something maybe right here," I indicated on the page, "but I am still not quite sure what it should look like. David was going to bring some samples, but he thought it might be helpful to stop in at one of the places that he usually buys from and take a look around to see if anything catches my eye. Maybe you and Grandma Rose could come with me early next week. What do you think?"

"We could come with you where? Hello, Paige," my Grandma Rose said, coming out onto the patio and sitting down beside me, patting me affectionately on the leg.

"Hi Grandma! I was just asking Grandpa if you two might want to come with me early next week to see if we can find a beautiful fountain for the garden," I showed her the sketches starting with the one that had the spot for the fountain.

"You and Grandpa should go. You don't need me there, I'll just be in the way," Grandma said, studying the sketches thoughtfully. She used a cane when she walked and she always thought it made her a nuisance to take in public, but it simply was not true.

"I would love your opinion too. You always have had such great taste. Plus, how can you resist wanting to spend time with your favorite granddaughter?" I said, smiling innocently at her.

"She'll come with us. Do you think your mom or dad would want to go with you though? I don't want to take that away from them if they were looking forward to it," Grandpa said, relooking at the sketches when Grandma was finished.

"Nope. They know the gardens are your territory. Mom and Auntie will be going shopping with me later next week to help start finding things for the guest rooms. Plus, I want to do this with the two of you!" I said, sitting back in my chair and sipping my iced cinnamon cold brew.

"Well then, we'll go," Grandma said, looking pleased. "We have a couple of doctors' appointments on Monday, but we could do either Tuesday or Wednesday."

"Okay, let me double check my calendar after I meet with David this afternoon and I'll call you so we can pick a time. Right now, I'm thinking Wednesday morning," I said.

"Make sure you show him all the pictures and if you have questions, just give us a call," Grandpa said standing up and handing me back the sketches so I could pack them in my folder. It was time for me to head out to meet my dad, and Grandpa was going to walk me to the door.

I put the folder in my bag and then tapped it gently. "I have all your notes right here, and I'll be sure to show the pictures to David as well. If there is anything he or I have questions about once we've walked the space, I'll give you a jingle." I kissed my grandma's cheek and then followed my grandpa into the house and to the front door. "Bye Grandpa, thank you for all your help with this." I kissed him on the cheek as well and he opened the door for me. "Think about what type of fountains you think would be pretty and have Grandma do the same. I'm excited to go shopping with you next week!"

"Love you!" I called loud enough so my grandma could hear it through the screen door.

"Me too," Grandpa said as I headed out and climbed into my car. I waved as I drove off, knowing he would be standing at the window watching me go. I originally thought about taking him to the meeting with me. It certainly would have made things easier rather than trying to remember all the details to convey to David, and then again when I inevitably had questions from David for my grandfather. But I really wanted everyone to see Hummingbird Hollow, in all its glory, once all the work was completed. I thought of how beautiful it was going to look as the final design took shape, everyone's fingerprints woven throughout the entire process, coming together to paint a one-of-a-kind picture that would have been impossible without each and every one of them.

That thought reminded me of another thing to do, so I pulled over at the top of the street and fished out my phone. I quickly read the text from my father telling me where to meet him, and fired off one back letting him know I was on my way. "Hey Siri," I said once I was back on the road. I waited for the pause in the music letting me know she was listening before continuing. "Set a reminder to pick up invitations at the store and also to ask Grandma Jane if we can have Christmas at Hummingbird Hollow this year." I thought it could be nice to have a couple of days that would be both a celebration, and a dress rehearsal before our paying guests started to arrive. I paused, trying to make sure there was nothing else I was forgetting. "Hey Siri? Please also add 'beg her until she says yes.'"

I knew it would add extra stress leading up to the big day, but I had been letting the idea roll around in my mind for the past couple of days while it took shape. It would be perfect. It would be my Christmas gift and thank you to everyone in the family. It would also make Grandma Jane's dream come to life for her. Our inn. With the fifteen guest rooms, it would be the perfect way to have everyone gathered for the first time in as long as I can remember. I would need to make a guest list once I had the invitations, and I needed to add 'Christmas programming' to my list of tasks to make it really special. Actually, Emily would be a great person to help with the events. I spoke to my administrative assistant, aka Siri, once more and had her send a text to Em telling her I had Christmas gifts for the whole family figured out, if she was willing to give me a couple of hours that weekend, and an open mind.

When I was back on the road, I called my dad. He picked up on the third ring, and I could tell by the sound coming through the phone that he was in his car. He answered with his usual, "Hello?"

To which I responded, "I'm starving."

"Hello Father, what a beautiful day it is today! And doesn't your voice sound so pleasant? Thank you for sending me the name of the restaurant and the address I'm to meet you at, that was incredibly thoughtful." My dad responded with a knowing tone in his voice.

"I'm sorry. Hello Father, the giver of my life. How delightful it is to hear you speak kind and loving words at me, your daughter. I apologize for my rude behavior, however I'm currently wasting away from hunger, and I fear the death knell may come before I've had a chance to reach you..." If he wanted dramatic, I'm always willing to oblige.

"Death knell, huh? Not too bad. You on your way?"

"Thank you, I try. Yes? No? Kind of? I may or may not have already forgotten which dining establishment I'm meant to be heading to, and now it would be quite unsafe for me to reread my text. You wouldn't want your favorite daughter to end up in a terrible car accident simply because you were unwilling to repeat yourself verbally, would you?" I asked him as I continued toward the inn. I knew my father would pick something in between him and the inn so that I could head there as soon as we were finished eating.

"I will tell you where we're going if you promise to dial down the dramatics just a smidge."

"Deal."

Hanging up, I turned on my music and gave myself the ten minutes it would take to get there to decompress and adjust my brain from work mode, to spending time with dad mode. The juggling of my family and the business was proving more difficult than I originally thought, but I was determined to keep a line between the two whenever possible.

Once we were seated and had ordered our burgers my dad asked me how everything was going. "I know we aren't going to spend lunch talking about it, but a dad has to ask," he said, taking a sip of his iced tea.

I let out a deep sigh, partially from being stressed, partially because I hadn't taken a deep breath in a while, and because it was helpful in buying me some time while I gathered my thoughts. "Truthfully? I'm all over the place. I mean, I'm one thousand percent over my head and have no idea what I'm doing. I feel like I mostly just keep taking steps forward because I don't know what else to do," I said while tearing the wrapper of my straw into teeny, tiny shreds. I fidget when I am stressed. I also happen to fidget when I am not stressed. I'm an all season fidgeter.

"Are you sorry you said yes to Grandma?" My dad was unable to keep a little bit of the concern he had out of his eyes.

I thought about it for a minute. "No. I'm not sorry I said yes, I'm just sorry I don't have more experience. I know Grandma has great plans for this property, and the entire family, and I feel like that is a lot of pressure. She's not putting it on me, but I'm definitely putting it on myself. And I don't care what you say, I know that you and Mom are worrying about me, and I don't want that to be the case either..." I paused as he started to shake his head.

"Your mother and I will always be worried about you, regardless of what you're doing. It's in the parent owner's manual and it's a requirement that you must agree to before they let you take the baby home from the hospital. So, you're just going to have to get over that part and not let it guide any of the decisions you are making. If at any point in time you feel too far out of your depths, you say the word and we help you identify an exit plan. Your mom knows it, your uncles know it, Grandma knows it. You may be doing a lot of the organization and work, but we are still all in this together as a family."

The waitress brought us our meals and we both dug in, with gusto, before continuing the conversation. I really was famished, and it would seem that my father might have been as well.

"Thanks, Dad. I know you, Mom, and everyone, would have my back. And really, Ben has been such a huge help to keep me feeling like I can actually accomplish this. But it's still nice to hear that my membership to the family won't be revoked if I end up needing to wave a white flag at some point. We aren't there though, just for the record. I really am pretty excited about some of the upcoming things too and I feel like getting all the right people hired was the biggest thing, so aside from inn staff, I think we're just about through that part of things."

We continued to eat and chat, allowing the subject of the inn to drop and picking up whatever topics we felt like discussing. It was much needed and very refreshing. We laughed a lot and continued to sit there, even after our meal was finished and paid for. Finally, my dad checked his watch and indicated it was time to head out. As he walked me to my car, I thanked him again for the pep talk. As I was climbing in, he handed me a notecard with a list of items on it.

"What's this?" I asked, reading over what looked like a weird grocery list.

"You mentioned you were going to run to the store after meeting with the landscape guy. I thought you might pick some of these items up for me while you're there, you know, since you're feeling better and capable and all that stuff now."

I gave him a suspicious look and said, "So, you're saying that because you gave me advice and bought me lunch, I have to run errands for you now?"

He smiled and nodded his head. "Yep."

"Wow. That's really low, Dad. Impressive, but low," I said laughing.

"That, my dear, is life. You're welcome," he said, grinning at me, kissing my forehead, then shutting my car door. "Have fun at the inn, we'll see you when you get home. Love you!"

"Love you!" I called through the closed door and window while laughing and shaking my head. "Parents." I mumbled under my breath in disbelief. It was time to get to

Hummingbird Hollow. I shook my head, gave one final wave, and drove out of the lot.

The meeting with David went even better than I expected. He was able to look through the sketches he had given me, as well as the images and notes I had from my grandfather and uncle and walked me through a plan that was also even better than I expected. We discussed timelines and I let him know I was attempting to do a pre-opening event for Christmas. I could tell that made him a little nervous because he mentioned to me that while he might not have everything one hundred percent completed, he thought we would be in good enough shape to make sure everything looked fantastic for the party. He let me know that he would make the couple of adjustments we discussed and get a quote to me before end of day, but that I should expect the number to go up a little bit from what I had been originally expecting. He also said he'd switch up the sketches and get them over to me digitally so that I could review them with Grandma Jane before signing the contract. Once all of that gets completed, and we send him a deposit, he will get started.

I looked at my watch to see how much time I'd have before Ben would join me. I was thinking about running a couple of the errands on my to-do list if I could. I sent him a quick text, and when he let me know he'd be by in a couple of hours, I headed back to my car. I threw the files for the landscaping in my bag, grabbed out the things I'd need when I met with Ben later, stuck those in the passenger seat of my car, then grabbed my purse to make sure I had my father's list in there. I had some shopping to do.

CHAPTER SIX

If it Ain't Broken... Give it Time

"I don't know how to make it work right now!" Emily yelled, her frustrations finally boiling to the surface.

"Well, that isn't going to work as an answer. I'm going to need you to know, or figure it out, or find someone to ask who does know. I don't care how it gets done, but it needs to get done, and I cannot be the one who deals with it to make it get done. You said you had this part, so have it!" I yelled back and then headed out the front door. I needed some air and a walk to calm down. The stress had been building like water against a dam for the past several days.

This final interaction was the thing that made the dam break, allowing the water to rush forward and destroy everything in its path.

I had returned home about fifteen minutes earlier, after another inspection at the inn. The inspection hadn't been unsuccessful, according to Ben, it just had given us a few areas we needed to finish before we'd get any further green lights. All I heard when he told me that was that the construction phase of this project, was never going to end. I had then walked in and found Emily and my parents sitting around the dining room table chatting and working on a puzzle.

Emily had come out for the week so that we could work together at refining the list of things that she had signed up to help with, and then she could focus on executing upon that list. One of the things on her to do list was bringing the Hollow into the technology world. She had been researching and making lists of the best systems and web design criteria to determine what was needed. It turned out that Bartender Bob was not only handsome and great at mixing drinks, but also a computer nerd. And since he and

Emily had been out on too-many-to-count-but-aren't-they-adorable-and-eek-I'm-so-excited-for-them dates, he agreed to help her out. Normally, when I was in a better mood, I'd point out lovingly that this inn was going to make a great wedding venue and that there would absolutely be family discounts for people like her and Bartender Bob, to which she would roll her eyes and say, "His name is CHAD, and we aren't getting married so calm down." I'd follow that up by reminding her that Bartender Bob actually loves his nickname and told me I could keep using it, so there. However. I was not in a better mood, so none of this took place. Instead, I went for a very long walk.

I knew it wasn't fair of me since I hadn't been home and seen the hours that Em had spent fighting with the website, or the tear-filled call she made to Bartender... Chad... or the reassurance that he would take a look the following day when he was off work, but I lost it. It looked like everyone but me had been having a lovely and relaxing afternoon. I had spent my whole day running around like a crazy person and was in desperate need of some help, and in that moment, I felt like I was completely in it alone.

The walk itself was helpful as it gave me time to cool down and remember that Emily was indeed there to help, and that it would do both of us a whole lot more good if we had an adult conversation about everything, instead of just shouting at each other. I headed back to the house to apologize for my outburst.

When I got inside, no one was at the dining room table anymore, although the puzzle was still out. I poked my head into the living room and saw my mom in the kitchen, and my dad in his chair. He didn't say anything, but he pointed up, letting me know that Emily had gone upstairs. I nodded my thanks then headed to the guest room where she was staying.

I made my way upstairs and knocked on her door. "Come in," she called.

I poked my head in the door before entering and saw her sitting on the bed, her laptop on her lap with papers and a couple books spread out around her.

"Hi," I said, heading into the room.

"Hi," she responded without looking up.

"I just came to say I'm sorry that I yelled," I headed over to the chair next to the bed and sat down. I wanted to say more, but decided to wait until she spoke, to see if she wanted to hear anything more or if she wanted me to leave.

She didn't immediately acknowledge the apology. "I have gotten a portion of the setup up done. Chad will be able to help me more tomorrow." She was still mad.

"Thank you, I appreciate it." I said standing to go, my frustration starting to eek its way back in. I understood that I shouldn't have yelled and that the stress I was feeling was not Emily's fault, but I had hoped that she might be understanding at the position I was in, and that she had also yelled. Either way, I knew that bringing any of that up at the moment, if she wasn't willing to have a conversation that acknowledged her part in the earlier interaction, would only lead to more yelling. When I made it all the way out the door, without any further comments from her, I knew I should just head to my room and shut the door, so that we could both have another minute alone.

I laid on my bed and closed my eyes for a minute. Emily and I were, almost, always really great at communication;

fighting was usually kept to a rare minimum. We were two very different people at our core though, so how we handled stress and confrontation, and even how we handled apologies, were not the same. So, when we did inevitably have a tussle, it usually took us a little more time to fully come down from it, because what the other needed might not be the first reaction.

I knew as I lay on the bed that Emily's response of heading upstairs and starting work on things again, was her nonverbal acknowledgement of my stress and apology for losing her temper. I was the type of person who needed to hear it though, so I felt unheard and unseen. This would keep my frustration higher for longer, which would in turn make Emily feel like she still needed to do something to show her behavior change; undoubtedly making her feel more frustrated because she'd already done what she thought I wanted, and it 'wasn't good enough'.

The truth was, while I might usually head back in the room to force the conversation, so that by the end we'd both feel better, I simply didn't have it in me to do it this time. I knew it was what I was supposed to do, but I just couldn't bring myself to do it. The list of things that needed to be done kept growing each day and I didn't have any more room to take on the things that others had already committed to delivering. I hadn't had a chance to fill Emily in on all the chaos, so she didn't have all the information she needed, and she loved a tighter timeline than I was ever comfortable with in real life, let alone situations like this. Her job demanded the ability to continue to make changes and keep things flexible up until the very last minute, so she had come by her ability to thrive at the eleventh hour honestly. For this particular project I had just hoped she would remember that I couldn't function that way and meet me where I was at. She wanted me to understand and meet her where she was, and I needed her to do the same for me.

A knock sounded on my door, and Emily poked her head in. "I just wanted to let you know I've done everything I can today, and I need Chad. He and I will work on it tomorrow before he goes to work. I know you're worried that I won't get it done, but I told you I would, and I will," she finished. I could still hear the frustration in her voice, and I sent up a little prayer to guard my mouth so that I didn't say something that I would regret later.

Taking a deep breath, I sat up. "I appreciate it. And I need you to know that it isn't that I don't know what you're capable of. I wouldn't have asked you to be a part of any of this if I didn't think you could do what you said you could. But I am really stressed out right now, and deadlines are not going great for me at the moment. You thrive in that fast-paced last-minute environment, I do not. So, I guess I'm just asking... I guess what I need right now is for you to know that I'm not capable at the moment of trusting any process from anyone—not just you—just because I trust the person. I'm in uncharted waters, and I need everyone to meet me where I'm at, because I cannot currently come to each of you. I know that might not sound fair, and I'm sorry for that, but it is the truth and I want to be honest with you, so you know where I am."

Emily thought for a minute and nodded. "I'm sorry I'm adding to the stress. That is never my intention. I promise you, I will get this done, and I will work harder at making sure you can see progress and know where I am in it. I am in this with you. Maybe not at the same level, but I am. So, tomorrow I will work with Bartender Bob..." she looked at me and raised her eyebrows emphasizing his nickname and letting me know we were good again, "and then when he goes to work, you and I will sit down and we will go over everything that has been done and what else needs to be done."

I nodded and indicated she should come and sit down. "Ben suggested we call a family meeting tomorrow night. I think maybe I push it one more day so that we can have a game plan. I don't want to burden everyone else with all this stuff," I said, gesturing to all the paperwork on the desk.

"I know you Paige, and I know you have meticulous lists upon lists for all the things that need to get done. You've worked timelines in eighteen different ways, and you have Ben and Grandma Jane, and your mom triple checking every scenario you have come up with. This is not from a lack of organization or detail. It's just a job that is too big for one person. Your family wants to help you. I want to help you. And if I remember correctly, you are always the first person who tells me that allowing someone to come alongside, and help is never a burden. It's a privilege that should not be removed from them if they want it. So, stop trying to protect us and allow us the gift of being able to help." Emily wrapped me in a bear hug. "I promise you this is going to work out."

I sniffled in her shirt, tears of relief at not being alone in the burden of trying to carry everything, mixed with exhaustion, started leaking out of my eyes. "So... would now be a good time to tell you about the surprise?" I said pulling away and smiling at her as though I just got caught with my hands in the cookie jar.

She squinted her eyes at me suspiciously and pulled back. "Surprise? There is a surprise?" I nodded. She shook her head, but did not look upset. "And what is this surprise?"

"Well, I thought it would be a really great idea, and a wonderful Christmas gift this year... because Christmas is so important, don't you think?" I said, trying to butter her up a little before continuing. "I mean it was supposed to be a surprise even for you, but now I just don't think I can pull that off, so..."

"I'm going to die of old age before you get to the surprise at this rate. What is it?"

"I may have somehow found a way to convince Grandma Jane that it would be a brilliant idea to host the family... like, the whole family—even Uncle Simon and Aunt Charlotte are flying in—at Hummingbird Hollow, for Christmas and New Year's..." I said finishing and having the smarts to look sheepish.

"So..." Emily said, trying to figure out the math of what I had just told her meant.

"So, I basically had a then brilliant, now potentially catastrophically stupid idea that results in great memories for the family if pulled off, by shaving about three weeks off the delivery timetable..." I said, doubt no longer creeping in at my idea but throwing open the door, waltzing into the room and making itself at home.

"Three weeks..." Emily said, the reality finally sinking in. At the look that must have crossed my face, she quickly changed her tone to be reassuring. "Some of our best, most memorable moments come out of those 'pretty stupid' ideas of yours... besides, this isn't even the same thing. You aren't in this alone, and Christmas with everyone together sounds like a once in a lifetime kind of idea. Hard work for sure. Tight timeline, indeed. But still a nice thing... besides, you do love to throw a party."

"It's because I'm certifiably insane. It's one of my many charms," I said, flopping back on the bed and putting a pillow over my face.

"That's the spirit!" Emily said, picking up another pillow and tossing it at me. "Okay, so since this new revelation does make our timelines a bit more... exciting, we both need to get back to work."

I sat up again, much less excited about the work part and much more excited about grilling her on Bartender Bob. "Is your boyfriend going to be able to fix everything with the website, reservation, and inventory systems?" I pulled the pillow off my head and made kissy faces at her, earning me another pillow shot to the gut.

"Yes, he is. And no, he's not my boyfriend. Or maybe he is, I don't know," she said. It was her turn to flop back dramatically on the bed and put one of the pillows over her face.

"So, you want him to be your boyfriend then!" I said, laying down and getting comfy, ready to hear all the latest. "Tell. Me. Everything."

"Aren't you supposed to be going somewhere important to do something incredibly time sensitive?" She was clearly determined to get out of the topic at hand. I looked at my watch and popped up off the bed.

"Egad! Yes. I am. Lucky guess. I would like you to know that this does not mean this conversation is over. I am incredibly single and seem to be staying that way for the foreseeable future, so it's only fair that I get the opportunity to live vicariously through you. Tonight. I'll sneak us some wine and tasty treats, then you can fill me in. Leave nothing out," I said, grabbing everything I needed off the desk while Emily stayed laying on the bed stretched out.

"No promises. Now get back to work, oh Shaver of the Timeline."

"I'm going, I'm going."

"See you for dinner," she called out as I headed out of the room.

"Make me something special!" I called back, heading downstairs and to my car, waving to my parents on the way out.

When I got back to the Hollow, things were pretty quiet. I checked my text messages and email to see if there was any information I missed. I had a voicemail I must have missed, from Ben's contractor friend Jake, letting me know that he had sent the crew home a little early so that he could rework a few of the plans in order to accommodate the inspector's notes from earlier that morning. He mentioned that he actually thought it could end up shaving some time off overall, and he recommended that I stay out of the main house until he got back the next day, or I would be depressed at the current look of things. I think his exact words were, "Don't panic, I promise it looks worse than it is."

Opting to take his advice, I decided to take a walk through the gardens. David had done a lot of the foundational work outside, so while the new plants were not yet placed, the pathways were redefined, and the old and dead things had been removed. Walking through the grounds, I was astonished to see how much of a difference the changes had made. I took a deep breath and sent a prayer of gratitude towards the heavens, finally feeling like I could see a little light at the end of a very long, very dark tunnel.

I decided to follow one of the main paths down to the pool area to check and see how that was coming along. Aside from the pool face lift, we had opted to add a couple of small seating areas and lounge chairs. The furniture would not be in for another week or so, but the area itself looked completely transformed. I breathed another deep sigh of relief.

I walked around the pool itself, which was still devoid of water, but it was gleaming with the new surfacing. When filled, it would make the water look like a gorgeous shade of turquoise. The tiling along the edges was also complete and added a Mediterranean flair to the whole feel. While the furniture was not out yet, it was easy to see where it would be set up based on the resurfacing of the area around the pool as well. David had partnered with a friend of his who restored pools and I was grateful for trusting him with it. Emily had been right earlier. I was not in this alone, and

I needed to remind myself that it was okay to lean on the others who were helping to make this dream of my grandma's a reality.

I had just started heading back up to the main house so that I could rearrange the rest of the afternoon, when David came around the corner, catching me by surprise. "David! Hi!" I said, a giant grin on my face.

"Hi Paige, I see you have seen the changes. What do you think?" He was gesturing to the pool area.

"It looks amazing! Thank you so much for your hard work. I was just getting ready to finish walking the gardens while I head back to the house."

"I'm glad you love it. I'm also glad you're here. I actually wanted to discuss something with you that we discovered when we were draining the pool and the jacuzzi."

My face immediately lost its enthusiasm. "Uh-oh. Why does that sentence simultaneously elicit fear in both my heart, and my checkbook?" I sensed the familiar feeling of stress, that I had temporarily left up at the main house, returning like it had just taken three shots of espresso.

"I promise you it's really not as foreboding as it sounds. We just found some stress fractures in the pool and jacuzzi, so we ended up doing a little more resurfacing than we originally thought. It has dried and we've started the sealing, but we are letting that cure before we add the water back in."

He knew I was waiting for the answer to two questions and he smiled. "It won't cost any more money because we always include a ten percent contingency in our estimations, so we're covered there. I did want to make sure you knew we're going to need an extra few days before filling the pool. Timeline-wise, we'll definitely be ready before the guests arrive in January, but we're going to be tight for Christmas Eve."

I didn't say anything and let him continue. "I'm hoping with some creative timing we can overlap the rest of the pool work with the garden work so that we can recoup some of that time. I just wanted to double check with you that you would be okay if we attempted to accomplish both at the same time, but assume that the gardens are the priority. I would of course keep you posted if that timeline started to be at risk."

It took me all of four seconds to agree. "Yes, I think that sounds like a plan. Prioritizing the gardens is the right thing to do, but I'd love it if we could accomplish both together. I know by crunching the timeline I have made your job more difficult, and I just want to say again that I am so grateful for everything you have done and are doing. With only a little over two weeks until Christmas, there isn't a lot of wiggle room left," I said, as we looked over the expanse of the property. "Thank you for letting me know, David. I really appreciate it. I know you still have a ton to do, so I will get out of your way. I hope you have a wonderful evening. I'd love to say don't work too hard, but I would not actually mean even a second of it, so I apologize for that," I said, starting back to the path that led to the main house and my car.

"Thank you for putting your faith in me, Paige. Have a wonderful night, and I promise we'll keep you posted. This is going to be a wonderful surprise for your family!" David headed back toward the pool area. He really was a great guy, and I was lucky to have hired him for this project.

With nothing left to do outside the main house, I decided I'd had enough of looking at broken or half completed things for the day and headed back to my car. I headed to a tiny little tea house that I had stumbled upon one day when I got lost. I ordered myself a pot of herbal tea and a scone, then spread out at one of the tables to start organizing the guest room themes and determine what each still needed in order to be complete. I figured it would ensure that the shopping weekend with my mom and aunt would be both enjoyable and productive, as well as keeping the overall look of each room a surprise since I could give them specific things to look for without them knowing where it would be going.

Both my aunt and my mom would need a bit of information in order to visualize what they were helping me find, so my plan was to paint a picture that was similar in layout but different in overall theme. I wasn't sure if it would be as helpful as I hoped it would, but it was the only plan I had, so I was sticking with it.

I scribbled and wrote notes, ideas, single words, and doodles. Anything that I thought could be helpful or inspirational in planning down to the smallest detail I could possibly think of. I even included the color of bath towels each room would have, and the scent of hand soap since scents illicit memories and I wanted each room to feel instead of just be.

"Would you like anything else?" The barista who had served me my small teapot asked, walking over to the table where I sat.

"Oh. Um, no thank you," I said, looking around and realizing the place had emptied out. It was also almost completely dark out the windows. The barista smiled and walked back to the counter as I looked at my watch and realized two hours had already passed. I quickly gathered my things, thanked her again, tossed a ten-dollar bill in the tip jar and headed back home.

When I parked in the driveway, I noticed that my sister's car was parked in front of the mailbox, which meant Holly and possibly Ben were joining us for dinner. "Honey, I'm home!" I called, walking through the front door.

"We're out here!" Holly called from the backyard. I paused at the coat closet to set my work bag and purse down before heading out the sliding glass door in the family room.

"Hi!" I said looking around and seeing my parents, Emily, and Holly. No Ben. The dogs came running over to greet me, and I bent over to pet them. "What are we doing out here?"

"We are making dinner," Holly said, standing in front of the grill, next to Emily and my dad, while my mom set the table.

"What are you making? It smells delicious. Where's Ben?" I asked feeling a little guilty. I hoped he wasn't missing dinner because of work having to do with the Hollow.

"We aren't telling you. You'll just have to wait until it's time to eat." Emily stated, answering the first question.

Holly answered the second question, "He's on his way. He wanted to take a quick shower, and I came straight from work."

"Okay good. I didn't want him to miss out on family night." I said, walking over and trying to take a peek at the grill before both Holly and Emily shooed me away. "What are you doing, Dad?" I said after sticking my tongue out at my sister and Em.

"I'm supervising. Go help your mother with the table," he said, letting me know he was not going to be helpful to my snooping.

"No need, I'm all done in there," Mom said, coming over and kissing me on the cheek. "I'm glad you're home. You look tired. Why don't you go get changed into something more comfortable, and then open some wine?"

I nodded in agreement and headed back inside, grabbing my bags to lug upstairs and then changed quickly, washed my face and pulled my hair back. By the time I got back downstairs, Ben was outside by the grill as well.

"White or red?" I asked, sticking my head out the slider. "Hey Ben! Are you helping with the..."

"Shhhh. Nope. Nice try," Holly said, putting her hand over Ben's mouth before he could accidentally tell me what was on the grill. "She's not to know what is over here, it's a surprise," she filled him in, and he nodded in agreement, then smiled and shrugged at me as if to say, 'Sorry sis, my loyalties are to my wife."

I stuck my tongue out at Holly once more and then refocused on the wine. "You know, I'd be better at picking out what to drink if I knew what we were going to consume..." I said, trying a different tactic.

"No dice," Emily said. "You hate white wine, so we all know we're getting red. Pick the one you like best." Dang it. Wasn't anyone going to help me out here?

"Fine, but I'm only pouring a glass for Mom and Dad. The rest of you traitors can just drink water." I mumbled under my breath.

"You better pour some for everyone if you want to eat tonight..." Emily said, a knowing smirk on her face.

"I don't like any of you," I said, heading back inside to do as I was told.

"How's it going out there?" My mom was waiting for me in the kitchen.

"Well, there are no firemen out there, so I'm going to say they're winning right now. Plus, Ben and Dad are overseeing everything so I'm hopeful that the mystery dinner will be edible and begrudgingly I'll add potentially delicious," I said, pouring wine in everyone's glasses.

Mom and I grabbed a couple of wine glasses each and headed back outside. "So..." I said, turning my attention to Holly. "Not that I'm complaining... I mean I was about being kept in the dark about dinner, but now I'm not... but to what do we owe the pleasure of your company this evening?"

"We wanted to see how things were going with the inn and we hadn't had dinner with you all since Thanksgiving," Holly answered.

"Didn't you just have breakfast on Sunday with Mom and Dad?" I asked, sitting down next to my mom and taking a sip of wine. Dang, that was good. I looked again at the bottle, committing the name to memory.

"I said we didn't have dinner. We always have breakfast," Holly said.

"Holly hasn't had a chance to go to the grocery store yet this week," Ben added before being swatted by his wife in the stomach.

"There it is. Now that makes sense," I said, offering the other glass I held to Ben.

"Besides, since you weren't at breakfast," Holly said ignoring both Ben and I, "we haven't bonded with you since Thanksgiving. Like Grandma Rose always says, 'I've practically forgotten what you look like!"

"You and I have been bonding for the past thirty plus years. And I saw Grandma Rose just last week when she helped me pick out a fountain. So, she and I are bonded, and she is very aware of what I look like."

"Ooh what did you get? Do you have pictures?" She stated, not really asking, more sort of pleading. I asked Ben to keep the designs of the inn close to the vest, so my sister hadn't seen much. Trying to surprise an entire family of people with a pension for wanting to know details was proving to be difficult.

"I'm not telling, and yes, but you cannot see them. It's beautiful though and totally perfect for the space. Grandpa is going to come out on Monday when the fountain is being delivered. He wants to see it installed. Grandma said she wants to wait until everything is completed."

"That'll be good. I'm glad the shopping went well and that you got to spend some quality time with them," my dad said coming over and grabbing his wine glass from my mom as she and I sat in a couple of the patio chairs.

"Me too. We had a lot of fun," I answered.

"Okay, dinner is just about ready," Emily said, starting to pull things off the grill. "Everyone go sit down."

My mom and I stood up to head inside and I whispered to her, "Do you know what we're eating?"

"No, they wouldn't tell me either. Emily and Holly really wanted it to be a surprise. Do you think we should be scared?"

I shrugged. "I think fear can be a very healthy thing. It keeps one's senses sharp."

"Alright, agreed," my mom said as she stepped in front of me and started walking to the kitchen like we were suddenly in some kind of race.

"You in a hurry all of the sudden?" I asked her, speeding to catch up.

"I don't know. I don't want to be last. On all those National Geographic shows its always the last one that gets eaten by the lions."

I looked at her like she was crazy, allowing her to gain more ground on me. "This isn't survival of the fittest, Mother. It's civilized dinner with your family," I said speeding up and cutting her off.

"Then why are you hurrying?" she asked, stepping in front of me again.

"I thought we agreed that the food was going to be delicious! When did we get worried that some sort of apex predator is going to come from behind and pick us off one at a time? Also, what happened to a mama protecting her cubs or fawns or babies or whatever at any cost?" I said, pulling out my chair and sitting down.

"That's when you're too young to defend yourself. You're a grownup. You've left the nest already. I mean I guess you've also come back, but whatever, all bets are off," my mom said, sitting down and helping herself to a healthy portion of salad. A contingency plan, no doubt.

"That's just rude, and I'm incredibly hurt," I said feigning insult and topping off our wine. Everyone else made their way in and based on the look on my dad and Ben's faces, the fake concern we had moments ago climbed a little. Something smelled just a little... off. "Holly tastes it first," I whispered to my mom before they were all in earshot. "She's lived longer, and she's been married, I still have so much life left to experience. Plus, if I never do get married, I'm the one who is supposed to take care of you and Daddy..."

"Deal," my mom said. We shook on it.

CHAPTER SEVEN

Extreme Makeover: Inn Edition

Saturday morning came bright and early. "Where do you think we should go first?" Mom asked while we were driving to my grandparents' house to pick up my aunt. We were in my mom's car since Phoebe didn't love having passengers in the back seat. They could fit in there, but it was snug, and they had to climb in from one of the two doors. My mom's crossover would be much more comfortable for everyone, and it would hold more than my little hatchback could.

I pulled out my list and started naming the local places that I thought could be helpful for both furniture and antiques. I liked the idea of shopping locally wherever I could, and I loved that the pieces we would find would feel really unique. From there if we needed to hit up any big box stores, we could.

We decided to stop and grab some lattes and muffins before getting underway. We'd need our energy for the day to come. Once we had enough for us, my aunt and uncle, and my grandparents, we headed to their house. It was definitely early, but we knew everyone in the house would be awake and dressed and this way we could spend some time with my uncle and my grandparents. We climbed out of the car, and I balanced the coffees while my mom grabbed the box of pastries and then went to ring the doorbell. "It's us," my mom called through the door. The dogs inside barked their early morning greeting and sniffed at the door excitedly. "Hi Abby! Hi Amy! Good morning, Maggie!" My mom greeted each one even though they couldn't see her yet.

My uncle answered the door, "Hey guys, good morning! Come on in."

"Hi Uncle Robert!" I said, carefully kissing him on the cheek while maintaining balance on the coffee.

"How are you, Paige? Here, let me help you," he said, taking the top tier of coffees.

"How was the drive?" My mom asked as we followed him into the great room of my grandparents' house. Everyone else was gathered around the dining room table.

"It was good. We got in yesterday afternoon," he said, setting down the cups and reading the names printed on the side, handing them out.

"Hello everyone," my mom and I said at the same time. We spent a few minutes catching up while munching on our pastries and sipping on our drinks. My grandpa told my mom about the fountain we found, forgetting it was supposed to be a surprise.

"Grandpa!" I said with mock sternness.

He giggled and shrugged. "I forgot. It's still going to be a surprise though; I haven't shown anyone pictures!" My grandmother just shook her head.

My aunt, mom, and I got up to take our leave. "Are you sure you don't want to come with, Grandma?" I asked. My grandpa and uncle were going to go play golf while we were shopping so my grandma planned to stay home with all of the dogs.

"Come with us Mom, it'll be fun," my aunt chimed in.

"No, no. I'm going to stay here with the dogs. It'll be nice and quiet, and I'll relax. You three go."

"Go with them, Ro," my grandpa encouraged, using his pet name for her.

"No, I don't want to go, I want to stay here. I'm fine. It gives me a chance to just sit outside, maybe take a nap or watch a movie or something."

"Okay. Well, we shouldn't be back too late. Do you guys want to all meet for dinner? We could go to that Thai place you love," my mom suggested. "Charles is just at the house doing some laundry before he goes and visits Jane, but he'll meet us too."

"That sounds nice," my grandma said.

"Just call when you are on your way back. We should be done around four," my uncle said, kissing my aunt goodbye.

We headed to the car and climbed in. I was going to do all the driving so that my mom and aunt could chat and review the lists I had for them. My mom filled her in on the plan while I pulled out of the driveway.

"If you grab that folder," I said as I pointed to the folder sticking out between the center console and the passenger seat. "I have a little packet in there for each of you. It's got rough sketches of the rooms and a master list of all the items we're on the hunt for."

Ben had helped make the sketches, so they looked more like blueprints than inspirational images. I needed someone in on the secret who could help me hide the theming ideas I had until the big reveal on Christmas Eve. Since Ben has been the biggest asset I've had in helping me with everything, it felt like he was the best choice. He and Jake were now the only two other people who had the entire vision of Hummingbird Hollow. It had been a great relief to see both of their faces as I filled them in on the details.

They were potentially more excited than I was to be a part of making it all happen.

I could tell my mom was a little confused at the drawings since there wasn't anything inspirational for design on them. "These look... nice?" My mom said, trying to hide her confusion.

"I know you were expecting paint colors and fabric swatches and everything, but I've been talking to Jake and Ben, and they were really helpful. They pointed out that aesthetics, while important, are not as important as making sure everything has the right proportions. They said it's the number one mistake young designers make." While part of that was true, Jake really had warned me to be mindful of sizing, the rest was a strategically placed fib to try to help explain the state of the drawings. It seemed to do the trick.

My aunt reviewed the list of items carefully. "Is there a reason these aren't broken up by room?" She asked when she reached the bottom.

"I thought it would be helpful to know quantities of what we needed. Don't worry, I have some ideas, but I really do want your opinions on what you like. I didn't want to put too many rules around what we were buying. I want you to feel unencumbered!" I said, maybe a little too enthusiastically. If they weren't suspicious before they definitely were now. Aside from my parents, my aunt and uncle were two of the people in my life who had always really understood me. They knew my personality, my flaws, my likes and dislikes. They knew when to push and challenge me and when to support me... my whole family did. This process was proving to me how close we all were, even when distance was a part of our lives.

I hadn't thought much about it beforehand, but I realized that with my aunt and uncle just finishing redesigning their own house, this shopping trip might be less fun for her. "Auntie, I'm so sorry! I hadn't thought about whether going house shopping for room décor would feel like a chore to you since you just spent months decorating your new house! I just thought it would be fun for the three of us to go out and spend some time together..."

"It's fine. I think we're going to have a great day. Besides, the inn and my house are very different, so it's actually really nice to have a bit of a change from what I've been looking for," she said from the back seat.

"We are picking out paint colors today too, yes? That should be fun," my mom said.

"Yes. I figured we could get paint samples today and take note of favorites. I'll take them to the inn tomorrow. Jake is supposed to meet me there to do a walkthrough and he offered to put patches on the walls to help me decide. Then I can get the colors to the painters, and they can pick it up!"

"Sounds like a plan. Do you want to get the paint samples first to help guide our décor choices or would you rather pick out some of the things on your list and end with paint?" My aunt asked.

"I was thinking maybe we start with the list? I'm not currently married to any particular color, and I thought we could let our treasures guide our paint choices."

"I agree. That way if we find something we cannot live without, we don't have to rethink paint," my mom finished.

Once we arrived at the first store, we started having a blast. We actually ended up spending most of our shopping time in that first store because we found so many great—and also so many absolutely horrific—things there. I was having the most fun I'd had in a very long time, and we were actually getting things accomplished. We found a lot of decorations for each of the rooms, including the bathrooms. Once we had covered every single inch of the store, we collected our bounty and moved on.

Throughout the course of the day we ordered all of the window treatments, found bedding, paint colors, decorations, and then finally began pricing out amenities like televisions, phones, alarm clocks and the like that would be standard in every room. At a couple of the places I snuck away to pay for a few extra pieces I knew would be perfect, and then had the managers hold them in the back for me until I could come back for them the next day so that my mom and aunt would be none the wiser.

At the very end of the day, we found an adorable little used bookstore and began rummaging through all sorts of different books. I wanted to make sure we had the library area ready and stocked with great classics and some kids' books that could be used to read our younger visitors to sleep at the end of the day.

Each of us split up in the bookstore and pulled out different things we found, piling them in the middle of the store to go through together at the end. We sat down on the floor and began sifting through our piles which may have been gargantuan due to my almost unhealthy love for books.

"Paige, are you really going to put these books in the library at the inn?" My mom was holding up a couple of cheesy romance paperbacks in either hand.

"No, I'm planning on putting those on my bookshelf. I figured while we're here... just set those to the side... and please note there are several more you're bound to come across. The one in your right hand is the first of a six-book series so..." I trailed off sheepishly. I mean... what did they expect from me in a store this cool?

"Look at this one I found. It's a complete history of the area. I was thinking that there might be a chance the inn is in here in its former glory," my aunt said, beginning to thumb through the pages.

"I mean that would be amazing if it was, but even if it wasn't I think it could be cool to have a book about the history of the area in the library..." I trailed off as my phone started to vibrate in my pocket. I set down the books I was holding in my hands and pulled my phone out to see who was calling. It was Emily.

"Hey, its Em. I'm going to take this real quick," I said as I tried to unearth myself from the books that had slowly buried me like quicksand.

"Well, hello pretty," I said answering my phone and heading to the front door.

"How do you feel about a mobile app?"

"Well, that depends, complete stranger, who hasn't given me any indication of who she is on the other end of this phone call. I'm afraid I am not able to answer that question right now as you could be referring to a variety of types of websites or apps, including those of a questionable nature, and then I'd be agreeing to something I do not morally believe in and also making myself susceptible to a whole bunch of shady information and dark web stuff through voice recognition..."

"We might be able to have the website be completely adaptable for a mobile app," Emily said.

"Why would I want a website or an app with a bunch of bad and most likely illegal information, for undoubtedly shady characters, if you, a total stranger, are so willing to either start a website or mobile app with me, a young and completely innocent girl you probably have never met before in your life?"

"I'm being serious," she responded.

"So are serial killers just before they strike. And focused too. Won't let anything deter them from their train of thought... are you a serial killer? Are you a crazy person disguising your voice to make me think that you are a nice girl, only to gain my trust, ask me to meet you at some seedy motel in the middle of nowhere, and then ax me?" I said, smiling and waving at the old woman who walked by with an extreme look of concern on her face.

"Fine. It's Emily. Emily Nettle. Your soon to be ex-best friend of almost twenty-five years whom you already called pretty when you answered your phone, which I'm assuming you don't say to anyone you don't know but whatever. Happy?"

"Emily!!! My very best friend in the whole world! How are you?"

"Why would you meet a stranger in a seedy motel in the first place?" Emily asked.

"I have no idea. If she was pretending to be nice, she could tell me there was a cat stuck in a tree, or a bird in a fireplace, and I would go to help get it out."

"Why would she be calling a complete stranger to help get a cat out of a tree?"

"Because all the firemen are busy with training Blaze, the firedog, how to run on a treadmill," I answered confidently.

"Who does that?" she asked. Now, it's probably important to point out that our friendship is based on a foundational rule that at absolutely no time whatsoever should Emily open up the gates to the carnival playground that is my mind unless she is prepared to pay the price.

Either she was not a quick study in this department, or today she had come to play.

"Either really bored firemen, or people with really fat dogs. Duh. Hey! We could put Blaze and the tree cat on the mobile app! You know, give us a philanthropic edge! Make people feel like we are there to support a community in need!" I said.

"There is no dog, and the tree cat was a ploy to get you to a motel to be murdered in your original story. Do you even know what philanthropic means?"

"Not a motel, a seedy motel... Philanthropic is 'the voluntary promotion of human welfare'. Thank you, college degree. And you've officially hurt Blaze's feelings and owe him an apology. Besides, who says my serial killer doesn't really have a cat stuck in a tree? Just because they are a bad seed doesn't automatically make them a liar."

"Actually, if someone is posing as a... never mind. Forget I even participated in the last five minutes of conversation. Chad is curious as to whether or not you'd like a mobile app. For now, it would be a place where people can learn about the inn, read reviews, sign the digital guest book... stuff like that. But eventually, we can tie into the reservation system so that they can check availability, make reservations, even see what events and experiences they would have access to. What do you think?" Emily asked.

"Wow, Bartender Bob is kind of amazing. You should really think about making that a thing. He's a catch. I like it. Except for the room reservation's part. I think I like the idea of our guests having to call and talk to a real human being. You know, keeping it a bit more personal in this ever-isolating world. I could be completely wrong, but I feel like it would be a really nice touch. Besides the B and B crowd doesn't really feel like a 'fly by the seat of their pants' in need of a quick booking at all hours of the night type of group."

"What do you mean?" Em asked.

"Well, it's not like us or my dad when he travels for work, booking at the very last minute without much forethought. He's looking for fast and forgettable. He isn't looking for charming and memorable."

"Interesting. Okay, well why don't I have Chad start working on some of it, and I'll ask him if he can get the reservation part ready to go without tying it in. That way if we decide we need it later, we can turn it on."

"Sounds good. I'll talk to Grandma Jane first thing on Monday and let her know. Hey Em? I think as the Operations Manager in charge of all things computer and technology related, you should be with Bartender Bob like the entire time he works on this... you know, to supervise."

"Supervising isn't going to suddenly turn him into my boyfriend, you know. And since when do I have a title?"

"Well, it certainly isn't going to get you anywhere with him with that attitude young lady. This is why Blaze doesn't trust you. As for the title, I figured you and I needed to sound official. Otherwise, what will they put on our little door placard outside our office? I'm the General Manager in charge of Guest and Community Relations. Sounds fancy, don't it?"

"Our office?" Emily asked.

"Yep. It's the Harry Potter closet under the stairs. It used to be a coat closet but with the renovation of the kitchen that Mrs. Morey did, it stopped being utilized in that way and became a catch-all for storing stuff. I figured we'd be okay sharing, you know, since we already pretty much share everything to begin with. But it's cozy. It has enough room for two grown-up desks and chairs. There is even some carpet space left over to cover in paperwork and make it look and feel like a real working office!" I answered.

"Wow, I'm impressed."

"Then my work here is finished. Gonna head back inside and finish sorting books for the library with Mom and Auntie."

"How many for you?"

"What? You think I'd waste time in this bookstore to find books for me to take home personally? I'm shocked and appalled by your accusation!" I answered, again waving and smiling at a concerned passerby.

There was complete silence on the other end of the phone.

"Only like eight... but in all fairness, some of them are a series so that's really like having only one book."

Emily just started laughing. "You are ridiculous and out of control. Talk tomorrow?"

"Tomorrow when I'm finished at the Hollow with Jake."

"Bye."

"Bye Em. And thank you... oh and Em?" I said.

"Yeah?"

"Next time you see Blaze, you really do owe him that apology... and a milk-bone."

"I'll get right on that at the imaginary pet supply store," she said and then hung up.

I headed back into the bookstore and resumed my position on the floor, quickly getting reburied under a pile of books. My mom had started a second pile of beautifully bound books that we could use as decoration in some of the rooms if we wanted to. I hadn't thought of that before, but loved the idea to help make the rooms feel cozy. Some of the book topics were wild, but since they were just for décor we didn't pay as much attention to that. Once we had all that we needed for the library, room staging, and personal reading pleasure, I went to pay for them while my mom and aunt loaded them into boxes the shop was nice enough to provide for us. As I loaded the boxes into the car with the rest of our newly purchased items, my mom and aunt both called home to let everyone know that we were just about finished for the day and could meet them for dinner.

Everyone met up about thirty minutes later and we had a wonderful meal. Everyone wanted to know what we had found so we regaled the group with our shopping adventure, including some of the stories that involved the most bizarre things we'd seen that day. Uncle Robert and Grandpa Frank told us how their golf game went, and my dad let us know that he was able to get all the Christmas lights up around the house.

"So, the whole house is decorated?" I asked sipping my hot tea.

"The whole outside of the house is decorated, yes. And, without incident, I might add," my dad said proudly. My dad had a habit of going through a lot of light bulbs from breakage when hanging the lights each year.

"Well, that will be very exciting to drive up to when we get home!" my mom said, happily.

After a while, the conversation drifted to a variety of topics, and I sat back and just took it all in. The weekend was turning out to be really amazing. My mom and aunt really came through and helped me get a lot accomplished. The house was going to feel like Christmas when we got home, which always made me feel happy. Jake and I were going to get all the paint colors sorted the following morning, and by the end of the week the Hollow would be painted and ready for furniture. The happiness I was feeling on the inside must have crept to my face in the form of a smile because Grandma Rose turned her attention to me. "What are you smiling about?" she whispered conspiratorially.

"Nothing specific really. I was just thinking that all of this is actually starting to come together and I'm so excited to be able to share it all with you. I think I just realized that we're actually going to be able to pull this whole thing off. It feels really good."

"You are the one who is making sure this gets pulled off," my dad said joining the conversation.

"But I'm only able to do it because of all of you. I would never be able to have gotten through everything we have gotten through without everyone's help. And on Tuesday Uncle Derrick will be here to help with the new signs and everything... it just feels like... I don't know. Like we as a family are building something pretty amazing. Remind me to thank Grandma Jane later... not until we actually finish the project of course, but after that. You know, for giving us all this chance. She made this possible."

"Grandma is going to be so proud... she already is," my dad said.

"I just feel like everyone is here. I mean everyone. All of you, but also Laurie and Grandpa and Nonni... everyone. It's like they're all a part of this place with us. I didn't realize how big it was going to be when I said yes, but I'm so glad I did. Hummingbird Hollow really is something that the entire family is a part of."

CHAPTER EIGHT

The Best Gift

I headed out to the Hollow early the following morning, stopping to grab Jake and I coffee on the way. He was waiting for me when I arrived, looking like a kid in a candy store as he stood on the front porch blocking the front door. "Good morning," I said smiling and handing him his coffee. "You look excited," I laughed as his grin got bigger.

"Good morning. Thank you for this," he said, indicating the steaming paper cup he was holding in his hand. "I know we have a lot to do this morning, but I wanted you to see how far things have come," he put his hand on the front door handle, but then paused again. I couldn't help it, I laughed. "Okay, last disclaimer, I promise. It's not complete. We're still very much going to need every single second of these final two weeks before Christmas Eve, but the walls are up. You can finally see exactly what it's going to be. Okay. Ready?"

I nodded, and he opened the door for me and stepped aside. My breath caught as I stepped foot into the foyer. Jake hadn't been kidding when he said that it was possible to see exactly what it was going to be. After weeks and weeks of construction and staring at open walls and beams, everywhere I looked was now closed up and ready for paint. Jake walked me through the whole ground floor and showed me the little details that had just been marks on a page prior to then. The hardware and finishes still needed to be put in, but overall, the inn looked magnificent. I couldn't stop staring. I couldn't wrap my mind around the fact that this was something that we created.

Jake watched me while I looked around, sensing that I needed a few minutes to take it all in. Finally, not being able to take it any longer, he broke the silence. "I know we haven't gotten to the guest rooms or the gardens yet, but what do you think?"

"It's... unbelievable." I said, at a loss for words. Jake hadn't yet seen the piles of things that were in the back of my mom's car, but they went even better than I could have imagined. "I just never thought it could be... this. And you haven't even seen what's in the car!" I couldn't help but have a little bit of shocked panic creeping into my voice.

Jake laughed. "I was wondering what happened to your Mini Cooper. I'm guessing the shopping trip was a success then?" he said, taking a sip of his coffee and leaning casually on one of the door frames, ready to hear what I had to say. It was then that I realized that my brother-in-law's friend was handsome. I mean like... handsome. I found myself nervous at his attention all of the sudden, and annoyed at myself for the sudden and inconvenient flutters that suddenly made my tongue forget how to work. Jake must have sensed something shift in me, although I was sending up silent but impassioned prayers that he wouldn't realize what it was, as well as mentally giving myself a pep talk to knock it off, stop acting like a schoolgirl and get it together. I didn't have time for a crush, and frankly the me I was about three minutes prior to realizing that Jake Kinnison was the precise type of man I could enjoy having a crush on, was the girl I preferred to be.

I shook my head to clear my thoughts and remember what he said. "I'm sorry?" I finally said, looking at him like I'd lost my mind. He chuckled again.

"I was just saying that I realized you hadn't brought your car when you came here this morning, so I'm assuming that means the shopping trip went well?" he repeated graciously. I was an idiot.

"Oh, yes. My mom's car was already loaded up from all the stops we made, so it made more sense. Plus, Phoebe, as cute as she is, just wouldn't be able to handle it."

"Phoebe?" Jake asked.

I could feel my cheeks flushing and taking on a bright pink hue. "Phoebe is my car..." I said, knowing there was no real way to explain why I—a complete and usually high functioning adult—felt the need to name... well everything. Including her car.

"Phoebe," Jake repeated as if trying it on for size. "I like it. I used to have a truck named Elvis, but he got totaled at a construction site a few years back. Long story. Haven't found the right name for this one just yet," he motioned in the direction of the parking lot, even though we couldn't see it from where we were. "Should we go take a look at the rooms upstairs and then we can start unloading everything? I'm assuming we have some paint samples to play with as well?"

"Sounds good," I said, keeping my words to a minimum and dragging my mind back to the task at hand. We had an inn to finish after all. "Oh!" I shouted suddenly, making Jake stop short on the stairs. "Sorry. Please don't fall and die because of me," I said in a rush. Jake laughed again and continued up the stairs when he saw I was still behind him. I continued, appreciating that it was easier to talk when I could concentrate on taking my own advice. "I forgot to tell you, I wasn't sure what to do about exterior paint and trim, so I don't have those samples. I was hoping you had ideas?" I asked, making it to the top of the stairs where Jake had turned to wait for me.

"Actually, I do. And I was even bold enough to get my own samples in the hopes that I might be able to convince you of my vision. I'll show you when we get back downstairs.

We toured each of the rooms, and seeing everything once again had me so excited the nerves I had been feeling earlier took their leave. I was so focused on what we were looking at and talking about, my brain graciously allowed me to go back to interacting with Jake the way I had before the bolt of lightning moment. I talked him through the furniture pieces that would be delivered once the painting was done, as well as some of the things we'd bought the day before. He seemed to be as excited as I was and asked a lot of questions.

We decided to move on from the house to the gardens before we started unloading the car and talking about paint. As we looked out over one of the main gardens where David had begun laying the stone paths and planters, Jake turned to me. "Okay I have a question," he said, pushing his hands in his pockets and admiring the expansive view.

"Ask away," I said, continuing to look around and breathe in the cool air.

"Why Hummingbird Hollow? I mean I love the name, don't get me wrong, I've just wondered where it came from."

I paused, unsure of how to explain it without it sounding cheesy. I took a breath and tried my best. "You haven't met her in person yet, but you know my best friend, Emily?" I said, finally turning my eyes to Jake and then regretting it instantly when I realized he was watching me intently as I explained. Cue the blushing of the cheeks and the butterflies in my stomach. I returned to looking out over the garden. "Her mom, Laurie. It might sound crazy, but she's in this place. I can feel her. When she was alive, she told me a story about how she would have loved to own a little cottage by the sea and call it Hummingbird Hollow. The first day I came here, I was really overwhelmed and I stepped toward the garden area to have a minute alone with God. I asked him to give me a sign that I was doing the right thing by saying yes to my grandmother's crazy idea. Just then two hummingbirds led me into the small garden right off the front of the main house and when I entered it, there must have been five or ten hummingbirds dancing through the flowers. It was so beautiful..." I trailed off for a moment, allowing myself to relive the secret moment God had given to me.

"I know it might sound crazy, but I think in that moment, I just knew. It was like this place was Laurie's last gift to help us continue and grow our story as a family... my grandma was just the one who grabbed ahold of the vision first, and was generous enough to share it with the rest of us."

Jake didn't say anything for a moment, making me wonder if I'd shared too much. "It's working, you know," he finally said.

"What is?" I asked, confused.

"Laurie's gift. God's vision for this family. You are all building something together; creating something that is going to be a piece of each of you. You've been spending more time as a family, growing closer, building new memories..." he paused for a moment before continuing, catching my eye and smiling brightly. "And you're bringing all of us along, allowing us to share a part of this whole family experience. Making room for others who need a family to be a part of... Emily, her sister, Ben... even me. So, I'd definitely say it's working."

I stood in reverence of the moment, a tear escaping my eye. I hadn't thought of any of that before. The gift that we had been given was growing with every moment of our acceptance of it; being shared with others. I couldn't even imagine how it could continue to grow and wrap around people who came to stay with us at the inn. Each and every person being brought into this family we had; this family that we were building with our own two hands; finding a place to belong even if just for a little while. Taking a piece of us and this place with them from that moment on. I looked at Jake in awe, finally understanding the magnitude of the bounty God had orchestrated on our behalf.

Jake seemed to understand because he just nodded and smiled and we stood there for a few minutes more, in silence, wonder, and gratitude for what was turning out to be the best gift.

We continued to work at the inn for the rest of the afternoon. We unloaded all of the boxes that I had brought with me, took out all the paint samples and painted patches on the walls in each of the rooms and tried very hard to not get any on the floors —of which we'd lifted up some of the protective paper covering to peek at—or on each other. Finally, when all that was finished, Jake walked me through his vision for the outside and it was perfect.

"I love it," I said, nodding my head as he explained it enthusiastically. "Ooh! What if..." I paused. The last thing I needed to be doing was adding another thing to the to do list. We were definitely getting there, but time was still very much winding down.

"No, don't do that. What were you going to say?" Jake said.

"I don't want to add anything else to the to-do list," I said still hesitating.

"Say it," he insisted

"Alright, alright. What if we were to hang..."

"Christmas lights?" Jake said, finishing my thought for me. "I'm so glad you asked! I was thinking the same thing.

I can hang them, and it won't be a problem at all. The only thing is you have to decide what you want. Clear white lights are very in these days, I've been told."

I laughed. Of course he'd have the same idea. The Christmas spirit was infectious here. "They would make the paint really stand out," I said, thinking.

"But?" Jake said, watching the wheels turn in my brain as I tried to picture the house lit up with the clear white lights. Don't get me wrong, they would be gorgeous. I just don't know if they say 'old time family Christmas.'

"But... I'm thinking maybe those old-fashioned colored light strands might feel more festive?"

"More like home," Jake said, looking at the main house again through the lens of the new light vision. "I think they'd be perfect." We both continued to stare at the main house envisioning it decorated for the holidays and how beautiful it would be. I was about to suggest a wreath for the front door, but Jake beat me to it. "What do you think about a large wreath on the front door and maybe some live garland going up the railing of the entrance steps. We could even wrap it around the porch railing," Jake said.

My eyes grew wide, and I stared at him in surprised realization. "Oh... my... goodness!" I said, starting to laugh. "You're a sucker for Christmas!"

Jake looked at me and looked slightly embarrassed. It was not a bad look on the man in the slightest. "You got me," he said shrugging and maybe even blushing a little. "I know I should do a better job at hiding it, but I am. I love Christmas. I love the music, the food, the decorations. All of it. I'm a complete and total sucker. And if you ever mention it to Ben, I will deny it with vigor," he said, finally laughing.

"Why would you deny it? I think it's wonderful. Christmas and everything it represents is the best time of the year hands down without a doubt. I love meeting someone who might just be able to match my enthusiasm for the holiday," I said. I sat on the top stair of the inn and looked out. "So, how do you feel about a giant Christmas tree in the foyer?" I leaned over and whispered as Jake joined me on the step.

When we were finished adding far too much Christmas decorating to the overall to do list, Jake stood up and helped me off the step. I had almost forgotten about the earlier visit of butterflies until they made a sudden reappearance at the touch of his hand on mine. I pulled away quickly, the surprise once again making me probably look like a complete crazy person. Jake was at least gentleman enough to not acknowledge my awkwardness, or he was completely unaware. I wasn't sure which one I was hoping for, I realized belatedly.

"So, what are your plans for the rest of the evening?" Jake asked casually while I locked up the inn with my key after we both made sure we had everything we needed from inside. He'd be back to work on another job site the following day but promised to come by and check in with the painters and David later in the week. The small talk helped ease me back into the comfort of colleague waters.

"I'm headed home after this for a quick cleanup and then heading to my sister's house for dinner," I said realizing based on the state of my clothing that I must look a horrific mess. I mean... that was fine. I didn't have time to fantasize about the type of women Jake Kinnison dated. Or if he was already dating; or would have an interest in someone like me... or if he'd just look at me like Ben did, as a fun little sister.

This. I didn't have time for any of this exact explosion of a thought spiral. I needed to focus.

"Oh yeah, Ben mentioned he was having some people over. Asked if I wanted to join," Jake mentioned. I dropped my car keys. He bent down to pick them up and handed them back to me. "You okay?" he asked.

No, I was mortified, but also a little relieved that he had actually noticed my weirdness. Not because I wanted him to notice of course, that part was completely, and embarrassingly, awful. Rather, I was relieved that he wasn't oblivious to... well... me I supposed.

"Sorry, yep. I'm just feeling a little... distracted. So, were you planning on coming?" I asked, stopping at my mom's car door.

"I told him I would. He was hoping we could bring him up to speed on everything we did here today and where we're at," Jake said. So, it would be a working dinner. Funny, my sister hadn't mentioned that part to me when she told me to come over for dinner.

"He did mention to you that we were all going to be there?" I asked, worried that the idea of meeting my entire family could be overwhelming.

"He did. I have actually been looking forward to it. It'll be nice to meet all of the people I've heard so much about."

"Good. We are quite the cast of characters, so I wouldn't want you to feel uncomfortable. I love my family, but like any family, we can be a handful to newcomers," I said. Jake leaned over and opened the car door for me. "So, I guess I'll see you in a little bit?" I said, hopping into the seat and setting my bag down on the passenger's seat.

"Yep. I'm going to head home and get cleaned up myself, and then I'll be there. Anything I can bring?"

I thought about it for a minute and realized I had no idea what my sister was planning for dinner. She told me just to make sure I was there by six. I knew my aunt and uncle were bringing Grandma and Grandpa. I assumed my mom, dad, Em and I would be picking up Grandma Jane since it was to be an entire family affair. "Honestly, I have no idea what the plan is, so I wouldn't worry about bringing anything... unless there is something specific you'd like to drink? I guess you could bring that," I shrugged.

"Okay, I'll see you there," Jake said, smiling and shutting my car door, then jogging over to his truck. I backed out of the parking spot and gave a little wave as Jake started his truck, and then headed home.

I called Emily first, since she was already at the house and would be able to be my hands and feet. She answered on the third ring. "Hi," she said sounding far too relaxed for my liking.

"I need a cute outfit, and a quick, but adorable hairstyle," I said in response. This clearly grabbed Emily's attention.

"Who is he?" she asked.

"Ugh. Jake. He got very handsome all of the sudden. And he loves Christmas, and he's very helpful, and I don't have time for any of this, and I'm going to kill my sister and brother-in-law, only not tonight because tonight I need to be... well not the girl in cargo pants, a tank top and a messy bun covered in sweat and dirt and fifteen different colors of paint."

"I have so many questions, but those can wait until later. I'll have everything ready by the time you get here. But then you will fill me in on how the contractor that you've been working with for the better part of a month has only just suddenly turned incredibly attractive," Emily said. From the sounds on her side of the call, I could tell she was already moving around in a way that let me know she was headed to my closet.

"I would like to know the exact same thing. It's fairly annoying and also incredibly inconvenient," I said. "I'll be home in fifteen minutes and then when I'm out of the shower, you can psychoanalyze my life as much as you feel led to. But only if you are simultaneously doing my hair."

"This is going to be fun."

"For whom exactly?"

"For everyone but you, obviously," Em said, hanging up the phone.

I immediately dialed my sister's number and when she answered she sounded far too sweet. That made me even more suspicious than I had been already.

"What have you done?" I asked without saying hello

"Hi Paige, whatever do you mean? How was your day at the inn with Jake?" Holly said, a smile in her voice. Yep. This was all her fault.

"Seriously sister, I do not have time for your meddling, so you better come clean. Like, right now. Or I will not be coming to dinner, and you will be uninvited to... everything I ever do for the rest of my natural born life."

"He's great, isn't he? Ben thinks you two work really well together, and with all the things you have in common..." Holly continued on as though she hadn't heard a word I said.

"Holly!" I said loudly into the phone, finally catching her attention.

"Okay, okay. Don't be mad. Really, we didn't mean anything by it, and we certainly aren't trying to meddle... much. We just both love Jake, and we love you, and we realized how much the two of you have in common, and then when Ben needed help and asked Jake to step in and it started going so well..."

I took a deep breath. I know they both meant well, and the truth was Jake had been a huge help so far and would probably be one of the biggest reasons this whole project got across the finish line. None of that changed the fact that the finish line was still rapidly approaching and needed my full and complete attention. "Holly," I said calmer now. "I love you. I love Ben. And Jake seems like a great guy. But I don't have time right now for any distractions. Frankly, neither does he!"

"Okay, so don't let it be a distraction," Holly said, as though it were the simplest thing in the world.

"Seriously? That's your whole pep talk?"

"Yep. That's it. You're both adults. You're working together; wonderfully I might add. So just keep doing that. It's just dinner, and Ben really does need to talk to you both. Plus, Jake has seemed really interested in getting to meet the family. He has been curious about who everyone is now that he's heard so much about them through Ben and the project." Holly said.

"So, just keep doing what I'm doing and ignore the attraction that may or may not have shown up suddenly this morning out of nowhere?" I asked, the wind leaving my sails.

"I mean, you could try to do that, but we both know attraction is not easy to ignore. Plus, I figure the more you try to fight it, the worse it'll be. So just let the attraction be what it is and put on your grownup pants and do what you gotta do to get the job done. There will be plenty of time for flirtatious giggles and smoldery looks later. Until then just let it be exactly what it is."

My sister could be infuriating, but she could also be right. The truth was, regardless of how caught off guard I felt about the sudden recollection that I'm a single female who is not immune to the ways of a gentleman, that knowledge didn't change anything. I needed Jake on this project. He wanted to be here. I enjoyed our time together and I wasn't ready to see it end. What if it really was that simple for now? "So what you're saying is you did me a favor, and I should be thankful?" I asked, the tiniest hint of a laugh in my voice. I took a deep breath.

"I like to think of it as Ben and I giving you an early Christmas gift," Holly said, her smugness coming through.

"A gift?"

"Yep. Like the best gift."

CHAPTER NINE

How To Succeed in Interviewing Without Really Trying

It was December seventeenth. Exactly one week left before my entire family was going to come and be the test and adjust crew for Hummingbird Hollow. I had spent the last three days interviewing for all of the staff positions, except for those that had anything to do with the kitchen. The chef auditions began the following day and I wanted to make sure that the chef had a say in their team.

Things had been going really well since, thankfully, I had been heavily involved in interviewing in my role at the restaurant. It wasn't all my interviewing prowess that had landed me the applicants I had the pleasure of meeting over the past few days. The recruitment company that had been recommended to me by Jennifer—my old boss and mentor who was happy to give me advice and recommendations when I needed some business insight—was amazing. She was also the one who recommended that I let the chef hire their staff to make sure the right mix was in play. "You know because you've lived it, but a restaurant staff that feels like family is wildly more successful than one that isn't a cohesive unit," she had told me on the phone when we spoke.

I was very happy with the offers I was going to make for the bell staff, reception desk, and valet team. I had also done several interviews for housekeeping and maintenance early that morning, and was now on a small break before my last two morning appointments. I was meeting my dad and my uncle Derrick for lunch to review the signage designs he'd developed for the inn. I pulled out my phone as I sat at my desk in the closet under the stairs and dialed my dad's number. He answered on the third ring. "Hi Dad, it's me," I said.

"What's up sweetie pie?"

"Well, you know how the interviews have been going really well this week and I'm getting ready to make offers."

"Yes, and I think it's great Paige. I'm assuming the references have also been what you're expecting?" he said.

"Yes, I'll be honest and say some are probably overqualified, but having a really strong opening team is not something I'm going to take for granted. Anyways, I was thinking that maybe you and Uncle Derrick could bring Grandma Jane with you to lunch if she doesn't already have other plans? I know she's ultimately leaving the hiring decisions to me, but I'd still like to run the top candidates by her and make sure she's on board with my choices and the size of each of the teams," a soft knock came on the open door and I looked up to see Jake standing in the hallway. He gave a smile and a small wave. I waved back and held up one finger and pointed to the phone to let him know I'd be with him in just a moment.

"I'd feel better making the offers if I knew Grandma was on the same page," I finished into the phone.

"I think that sounds like a great idea. I'll call her as soon as you and I are off the phone and make sure she's not otherwise engaged," my dad said.

"Thanks, Dad. How is everything else going?" I asked.

"Great. Derrick has shown me the sketches for the signage at the Hollow and I think you're going to really love them."

"I cannot wait to see them. Ben texted earlier and said they were pretty amazing. Jake just got here, so I have to go in a second, but I had another idea last night and I wanted to get your take on it," I said, motioning to Jake to come into the office and sit down at Emily's desk until I was done.

"I'd love to hear it. What's the idea?" Dad said.

"I was just thinking that I really wanted to do something a little different than other bed and breakfast locations I have researched. I want to make sure we give our guests something memorable as a token of our appreciation for their patronage."

"So far, so good," my dad said encouragingly, while Jake gave a thumbs up while he played with one of the fidget toys I'd accidentally left on Emily's desk.

"I was also thinking that it should be something that could be a little different each time they came so that it felt unique and special even if they were repeat visitors... So I was thinking, what if I hired an in-house sketch artist? We could get a photograph of the guests or take a photo of them, and then we could have the artist pencil sketch them into a Victorian era setting with Hummingbird Hollow in the background. I figured it could change based on seasons and holidays, allowing not only for a different sketch each time, but also a kind of timeline for our guests who feature each year. It wouldn't be cartoony or cheesy, just a beautiful five-by-seven pencil-sketched portrait to commemorate their time with us..." I trailed off, starting to feel self-conscious of the idea now that I'd said it out loud. Maybe it was too cheesy and unrealistic; something that was just an added expense for the inn without any real reason.

Jake had stopped fidgeting and was just looking at me with an unreadable expression on his face. My dad was quiet for a minute before responding. "I think that sounds like a very interesting idea," he said cautiously. "But how would you get their photograph? Why not just offer them the sitting with the artist in the first place?" My dad asked.

"I thought about that, but then I thought a lot of our guests were probably going to be on some sort of timeline. Whether that be antiquing or sightseeing. Sitting for the sketch would take time away from their agenda. Plus, I thought it could be a surprise gift that was waiting for them at the front desk when they were checking out. Plus, if we got the photos ahead of time, it would allow the artist to sketch on his or her timeline and not have to work weird hours. I thought maybe Uncle Derrick could help me find the artist while he was here."

"Okay, so walk me through how that would work," my dad said, putting on his practicality hat. I was trying to not let the logistics deflate my enthusiasm because I knew that was not what my father was intending to do.

"Okay so you and Mom are going to be guests at the inn, and you are checking in tomorrow. You arrive and you are welcomed by me at the main reception area, and while I'm checking you in, Susie the hostess asks to take your photo..." I say, working through the vision in my head.

"I ask Susie what she needs a photo of us for and she says?" my dad said walking through the vision with me.

I think for a moment, allowing the question to run around in my head for a moment. "She says that it is for our guestbook. Because we like to include small images of the people who have stayed with us next to their guest book entries."

"Did you just make that up?" Jake asked out loud, no longer able to keep his interest hidden.

"Was that Jake?" my dad asked.

"Hello, sir. Yes, it's me," Jake said, leaning towards the phone.

"Yes, I did just make that up. Is it dumb?" I asked both men at the same time.

"No, I actually think it's kind of brilliant, because the guest book will then be a keepsake for your family and everyone involved has something special that ties them together," Jake said, leaning back in his chair.

"I agree," my dad said from the phone.

"Really? It's not dumb?" I asked.

"I don't think it's dumb at all, sweetie," my dad said. "If that was your mom, she would say 'Oh Charles, we have to be in the book. Hang on does my hair look alright? I need to add some lipstick...'" all of which was probably exactly how it would go.

"So, then Susie takes your photo and shows it to you to make sure Mom approves," I said, walking through the rest of the scenario. "And then she thanks you and calls Seymour over to take your bags and escort you to your room." I finished.

"Seymour?" Jake asked.

"First name that popped into my head," I shrugged.

"Seymour is the first name that popped into your head?" Jake said, shaking his head.

"So not the point," I responded

"Fair enough. Please continue," he said, his eyes dancing with laughter.

"Thank you. So, Seymour takes Mom and Dad up to their room and then I email the photo to the artist who has no name so you can stay focused—thank you very much—

and then based on check out dates, the artist can prioritize the sketches. We can create a studio on the premises if they want one, or they can work from their studio if they already have one. Anyway, said artist finishes the sketch however they want..."

"While your mother and I are off just enjoying our vacation," my dad added.

"Yep, and then on the day of your checkout, you'll come down for breakfast and you'll check out and at that point in time Chelsea will hand you..."

"Wait, who is Chelsea?" Jake asked.

"Chelsea is the hostess at the front desk," I respond as though it's the most obvious thing in the world.

"I thought Susie was the hostess at the front desk."

"Susie gets days off, I'm not a slave driver. So, Chelsea is working the front desk at the moment. Also, still not the point," I said sternly but I couldn't help but let a smile creep onto my face. "So. Chelsea has you sign the guest book, and you see your photo in there and you think we're the bee's knees. And then Seymour who is not currently on one of his appointed days off helps take your luggage to the car right after Chelsea hands you a small envelope that you think is most likely a copy of your bill, so you hand it to Mom who opens it immediately and then starts crying when she sees the sketch."

"I love it. Run it by your grandmother at lunch. Now go help Jake so you can get back to your interviews!" My dad laughed and we said our goodbyes and ended the call. I turned my attention to Jake.

"I love it too, for the record," he started, smiling at me. "I also like that you are a nice boss who believes in giving your fake employees days off. That'll really help with morale."

I couldn't help but laugh again. "What can I do for you," I started and then glimpsed at the clock on my phone, "in exactly twelve minutes or less?" I finished, smiling sweetly.

"Kind, but tough boss. Also a trait I appreciate. I just wanted you to know I'm heading to my other job site for the rest of the day, but I'll be back tomorrow to finish with the Christmas lights and garland, so bring your Santa's helper hat."

"Sounds good. Thank you again... for everything Jake," I said, standing up to walk with him to the front door. The two of us had fallen into a comfortable rhythm since dinner at my sister's house. We both knew what was at stake and were determined to keep our eyes on the prize. It didn't mean I didn't enjoy our banter and time together when we had it.

As we walked to the front door, we saw a car pull into the lot. "Looks like your next interview is here, so I'll let you get back to it. You know where to find me if you need anything," Jake said.

It gave me an idea. "Hey, if you mean that, could I borrow you for about an hour tomorrow morning before your Christmas Elf work begins? I would love it if you could take a look at the applicants I have for the maintenance team and tell me what you think."

"I'll bring the coffee," he said smiling and opening the door to the young woman walking up the front steps. "See you tomorrow morning." He winked and then was gone before the blush had a chance to finish blooming across my cheeks.

"Cameron?" I asked as the woman standing in front of me smiled. "Welcome to Hummingbird Hollow," I said, leading her to the dining room to get the interview underway.

The interview went very similarly to the others. Cameron was pretty amazing. She was incredibly organized and had all the qualifications I was looking for. She was also incredibly nice. I made sure to put a star next to her name so that I could remember later that day to follow up on her references. She was going to be a great asset to the front desk and guest services team.

The next interview didn't go nearly as well. He wasn't quite the fit I was looking for, but the kid was nice enough. His name was Nathan, and he was the younger brother of one of the applicants I had interviewed earlier in the week. This would be Nathan's very first job and I could just see the nerves pouring off him from the very start.

Nathan struggled answering the questions and didn't seem to have any skills that were pertinent to the inn itself. Or rather, if he did, he didn't talk about them, no matter how I phrased the questions. By the time I thanked him for coming in and speaking to me, after a full twenty minutes of torture, he bolted out of the chair and was to the front door before I could get to my feet. He seemed to have a change of heart at the last minute and turned as he opened the door.

"Sorry, that probably wasn't the best way to end an interview..." he mumbled, mentally berating himself for the thousandth time since I'd met him.

"It's probably not something that I would make a habit of every time you interview," I said smiling. "But it is absolutely okay to be nervous sometimes. Most of us are, even when we have done a lot of interviews."

"I'm probably not getting the job, am I?" he asked.

"Do you honestly really want it?" I asked as gently as I could. "I mean, it doesn't feel like a place you'd want to be. You'd have to be talking to guests all of the time."

"I promised my mom I'd come down. I wanted to get a job with the school. In the library, actually. Books don't talk back, so I'm pretty comfortable with them."

I smiled and walked over to where he was standing. "I think that the library would be a great job. And hey, I can come in every now and again and ask for recommendations for this place, which would be a great help."

He smiled shyly at me and nodded his head.

"It was very nice meeting you, Nathan. Don't be too hard on yourself all the time. I have a feeling you have quite a few talents worth getting to know, as long as you don't sell yourself short."

He just shrugged his shoulders and gave me another half smile. "Thank you for your time, Ms. Donovan."

I involuntarily flinched at that a little. Geez. I'd never been a Ms. Donovan to anyone. Weird. "Please, call me Paige. Have a good day, Nathan. And good luck with the library!"

He headed out the door and gave a little wave as he went down the steps toward his car. I couldn't help but smile and shake my head a little as I shut the door. I had forgotten the lesson I had learned at my old job until that moment. Sometimes, the person least qualified for the job was the one you ended up rooting for the most.

CHAPTER TEN

How do you Solve a Problem like Maria?

As soon as Nathan was out of sight, I closed the door and headed back to the office to grab my things. I locked up the office behind me and made my way to my car. I had one stop to make before I met everyone for lunch. I headed down the driveway—waving to David and his team as I went—and then headed toward the local paper company.

My Grandpa Frank and his brother were printers in their younger days, and I always had a soft spot for beautifully crafted paper goods and personalized and unique fonts and prints for letters or invitations. I loved it when Jennifer let me take over the reprinting of menus by season and worked with a local paper goods company to ensure the menus were as themed and beautiful as the food that our chef had curated.

I pulled into a parking spot right outside the small but adorable storefront and headed inside. There was a soft bell that tinkled when I walked in, letting the paper fairies that owned the shop know about my arrival. I headed to the old post office sorter that had been adorably repurposed to create a sales counter while still highlighting some of the bits and bobs that could make excellent last-minute purchases. A girl probably around seventeen years old was sitting behind the counter looking incredibly bored as she played with a pile of paper clips and blew bubbles with her gum. She did at least look up as I entered the store, so that was something I supposed.

Her name tag clearly had different feelings than the woman it was pinned to, since it read in cheery bright letters 'Hello! My Name is MARIA and I'm Happy to Help!'. I set my purse gently on the counter and pulled out a folded piece of paper. All the while, Hello! My name is MARIA continued playing with her paper clips and snapping her gum.

"Hello," I said, smiling. I was hopeful that once Maria had something more exciting to do than giving paper clips a massage, her friendly personality would make an appearance. Apparently, I was only partially correct in my hope. While she didn't acknowledge me verbally in any way, she did cease the bubblegum Olympics and make eye contact. I'd take it.

"I'm here to meet Dolores?" I said, hoping that the riveting interaction I was currently having mostly with myself would be able to come to an end as quickly as possible. "She and I spoke on the phone, and she let me know to stop by today to approve the design on some invitations I'm ordering so..." I trailed off. I was fairly certain this young woman did not care why I was here.

"Dolores isn't in yet. She'll be here later this afternoon. She had some sort of appointment or something. She asked if I could be a 'dear' and open the store for her. I don't know why other than she and my mom are friends, so my mom told me I had to," she let out a dramatic sigh. If I were being honest, I wasn't sure what to do with the overshare that just occurred. She returned her attention to her paper clip pile.

"I'm sorry to hear that. Do you happen to know if Dolores left the print somewhere so that I can approve it?" I knew it would probably have been simpler for me to just leave and come back when Dolores returned, but my afternoon was pretty packed and I was already creating a tight deadline for pickup as it was.

Maria blew one more bubble and then took a deep breath. "Name?" She asked.

"Paige. Paige Donovan?" I said, again hopefully. Maria nodded and then pulled herself off the chair, finally seeming like she was ready to help.

"I believe Ms. Dolores has it in the back. I'll go get it," she said and then headed quickly to a door in the back of the room.

I looked around the store while Maria was gone, and made a note to come back and spend some more time when Dolores was working. There were a few ideas that I thought could be great, like the guestbook and the paper for the sketches as gifts. Menus could also be designed from some beautiful linen paper I saw on one of the displays.

Maria came back a few minutes later, her eyes a little puffy, but carrying a paper box with something taped on the top. She handed it over so that I could see the proof on top and then quietly said, "I'm sorry for... before."

I stopped reviewing the invitation in front of me, which—from what little I had seen—already looked better than I had imagined. "Everyone is allowed to have a bad day once in a while," I said, smiling kindly at her. I didn't really know how else I could help, but I did remember that being a seventeen-year-old girl was complicated and everything felt very big at that age.

"I was supposed to be spending the day with my boyfriend, but then Ms. Dolores called and my mom told me I needed to help out here instead. It's not that I usually mind lending a hand at the store, I mean Ms. Dolores is wonderful and she rarely asks for anyone to help her with anything it's just... now my boyfriend is mad at me and he won't answer my texts, and..." her eyes started to well up a little again, and she swiped at them angrily. "And none of this is any of your concern because you are a complete stranger who just wants to place an order for some beautiful invitations," she said trailing off.

I couldn't help it, I was growing a soft spot for Hello! My Name is MARIA!. "You're right, we don't know each other, at all. And I am here to review this proof," I said looking back down and finalizing the review, "which is absolutely stunning, by the way. Please tell Dolores that everything is better than I imagined and I'll be by at the end of the week to pick the order up. I have a few other business items I'd like to discuss with her then as well. But all that being said, I do know that relationships can be complicated. I also know that it will work out. Give your boyfriend a little time. If he's really mad, he's not being fair to you, and he needs to get over it. Pointing that out to him isn't going to be helpful though," I added at the last minute

"If he's not really mad, and he's just disappointed that he doesn't get to see you, he'll come around. In the meantime, you're here to help Ms. Dolores out. Imagine how upset she'll be when she learns that you've been miserable and fighting with your boyfriend because of her," I said, again smiling at Maria.

She took a deep breath and nodded her head, wiping her eyes on her shirtsleeve, and then tucking her phone into her back pocket. "Thank you, Ms. Donavan. You've been very kind. I'll get this order rung up for your right away, and I'll make sure Ms. Dolores knows you'll be back on Friday."

When the order was paid for, I gave Maria's hand an encouraging squeeze before heading out the door. Oh, to be seventeen and in first love again. I smiled to myself and then looked at my watch. Fiddlesticks, I was running late and needed to get to lunch.

When I arrived, everyone else, including my grandmother, was already seated. It looked like Ben was able to join us as well, which was a pleasant surprise. I rushed over to the table, unbuttoning my coat and tossing it over the back of the chair as I quickly sat down. "I'm so sorry I am late! I got a little hung up at the paper..." I trailed off suddenly, remembering the invitations were meant to be a surprise. Smooth, Paige. Really smooth.

My dad looked up over his menu. "The paper...?" He said, his curiosity peaked. Leave it to him to actually be listening the one time I was hoping he was more interested in figuring out what he wanted to eat. I had to recover quickly since Ben just leaned his head further into his menu. Thanks for the help, brother dearest. I thought.

"Sorry, the Paper Company," I said. "It's a charming little shop down on Main St. that I discovered a couple months back. Anyways, I was there because..." I opened my menu pretending to take a good look at it to buy myself time for the words to come, "I thought they could be a good place to start for some of the items we need for the Hollow. Like the menu printing and the idea, we discussed earlier," I said finally able to make eye contact with my dad. That was close. I didn't want to have to lie about the surprise, but I didn't want to blow it either. When Ben met my eyes and winked, I knew I covered well. I also stuck my tongue out at him for not coming to my rescue.

"That sounds nice," Grandma said, putting her menu down. "What idea did you two discuss earlier?"

Before I could fill her in, a young girl in her early twenties walked over to the table. "Hello, my name is Maria and I'll be your server today. Can I get you started on some drinks while you look over the menu?" she said. I dropped my menu before recovering.

"I'm sorry did you say Maria?" I asked, thinking that maybe I had imagined it. This Maria didn't seem to be much more enthusiastic than the original.

"Yes, I did?" she said, her voice pitching a little higher at the end as she trailed off, creating a question instead of a statement. A worried look crossed her face as she held her pen poised on her order pad. I shook my head quickly, to bring myself and my manners back to the present moment.

"Sorry," I said, smiling at her. "It's just been a weird day for me. Would it be possible to get an iced tea?" I asked, trying to get us back on track. 'Hello, my name is Maria' the Second smiled and relaxed a little. She probably surmised that I was just a little quirky but seemed harmless enough.

Since everyone else at the table had drinks, Maria tucked her order pad into her apron and said, "Sure thing. I'll be right back with that, and to take your orders." She turned and headed toward the kitchen. I went back to looking over the menu so that I'd be ready to order by the time Maria the Second returned.

"What is everyone eating?" I asked hoping someone's choice could be inspiration for me.

"I'm getting chicken tenders," Grandma Jane answered definitively.

"Tuna melt for me," Dad said.

"I think I'm leaning toward a chicken pot pie," my Uncle Derrick said, still looking contemplative. "I haven't had one of those in a really long time and it says it's a specialty. Homemade crust really does make all the difference."

"I'm getting a burger," Ben said. "Potentially with onion rings. How about you? What are you thinking?"

"I'm thinking the tomato bisque and grilled cheese," I said, perusing the menu one last time to be sure before closing it and setting it down. If I kept looking, I was bound to change my mind another half dozen times.

Maria came back and brought my iced tea and then took our orders. Once she had cleared all the menus, I turned my attention to my Uncle Derrick. "Ok, I know we have a lot to cover today, but I was hoping we could start with the sign. I've been told its pretty amazing."

Uncle Derrick pulled out a folder from the empty chair next to him and opened it up, sliding an oversized piece of paper out of it and then handing it over to me. I knew that it was only a sign, but it really was absolutely gorgeous. The lettering was classic and elegant, but would still be legible from a distance. There was an oval pattern made out of what looked like very intricate vines or leaves that circled the writing, and in the top right-hand corner of the oval—if ovals had corners, of course—there was a large hummingbird with three smaller hummingbirds around it. The birds themselves had so much detail to each of them that they looked like you could reach out and touch them. He had somehow created a blurring effect around their wings so that they also looked like they were really flying, and the flutter was at a speed that was simply too fast for the average eye to register.

I ran my fingers over the sketch. "It's beautiful. It really is perfect." I looked over to my uncle before handing the sketch carefully to my grandmother. I knew she'd already seen it, but I thought she might want to view it one more time. "Thank you so much for this. You did so much more than I could have ever imagined. Every time I look at it, I'll think of you. I'm assuming you'll be there to oversee the install, is that a fair assumption?" I knew my uncle liked to see things through from concept to completion.

"I'll be there. I have to make sure it isn't hung upside down, or lopsided or backwards or anything weird like that," he said laughing. I knew that Ben and Jake were most likely going to end up being the two doing the install so there was very little chance of it not being perfect, but my uncle would enjoy being with them and neither man would mind having him there.

"Well then. Now that we have that settled, would you all like to move on to talking about hiring?" I said over-enthusiastically.

"Actually, I was hoping we could circle back to the idea you were discussing with your father earlier today before we get into the hiring discussion," my grandmother said taking a sip of her soda. That woman never missed a thing.

I nodded and got ready to start explaining my idea for the patronage gift, but before I could, Maria came to see if we needed refills on any of our drinks. Something must have happened mid-step, however, because before she could stop to ask, her feet, having a mind of their own, continued forward. There was simply no better way to state it: Maria walked directly into the table. Drinks tipped over and spilled or sloshed onto the table.

Startled, Maria set down the pitcher in her hand to try to help, but ended up tipping that over as well, so it spilled onto the floor. Thankfully Ben and I both had catlike reflexes and the sketch of the sign and our cell phones were all snatched up without serious damage being done.

"Ohmigoodness! I am so sorry! I'm such a klutz! I'll go get something to clean all this up," Maria said scurrying off in a fluster to get towels and such to clean up the mess. Fortunately, aside from the table and floor the only other things that were in the path of all the liquid were my uncle's pants and shoes.

I felt terrible, both for my uncle, and also for Maria the Second, who it would seem was having the same no-good-very-bad-day as Maria the First. Maria came back quickly and wiped everything on the table, very nearly knocking another glass over in the process. One of the bus boys came and mopped up the floor thoroughly to ensure the ground wasn't sticky and that none of us slipped. Once everything was clean and dry—and Maria promised to comp my uncle's meal and all the drinks for the table—she went to check on our food.

Uncle Derrick slid the sketch back into the folder and placed it safely in his bag on the chair. Once everyone was settled—and the food in front of us and drinks were replaced—we got back to the subject matter at hand. My grandmother loved the idea of the sketches, and Uncle Derrick thought he might know of the perfect local artist for the job. He let me know that he'd reach out later that afternoon and keep me posted on how the conversation went. We finished our food and waited for Maria to clear the table before we allowed the topic to turn to hiring decisions.

It was my turn to pull out a folder from my bag and set it in front of me, pulling out the stack of papers and handing them over to my grandmother. One by one we reviewed the candidates. I provided details from the interviews and the reference conversations while they reviewed the résumés and the completed applications. They asked all the questions they wanted to and then after everyone had a feel for their top candidate, I would let them know who my top pick was. If there was disagreement—which there was surprisingly little of—we'd discuss further and determine how to proceed. When a tie breaker was needed, my grandmother would get the deciding vote. The entire process took a while, so by the time we were through all of them, we were anxious to get going and not hold up the table any longer. As I started packing up, my grandmother spoke up. "We have just one more thing to discuss before we all go our separate ways. Paige, you'll want to keep that folder out for just a moment longer."

I looked around to see if anyone knew what she was talking about. Uncle Derrick and Ben looked as befuddled as I did, but my father looked suspiciously unsurprised at my grandmother's statement. She continued. "Charles, hand me the envelope I gave you when we got out of the car," she said, reaching her hand toward him. He handed her a legal sized envelope that he produced out of the inner pocket of his jacket. My grandmother reached across the table and handed it to me. I took it from her and turned it over in my hands.

"What is this?" I asked her, trying to rapidly run through the list of things I could have missed doing that she would have had to step in and do due to my misstep. I could think of nothing.

"It is the name of someone I'd like you to hire for the front desk team. She is the granddaughter of one of my friends, Sophia. I have met her a few times, and she seems like a very nice girl. Sophia has been worried about her with the way the economy has been. She hasn't been able to find herself a job, even though she has been trying for a while now. I think that we can help her, and I would like to do so."

I hesitated opening the envelope, and instead set it on the table in front of me. I was feeling a little uncomfortable at the request—and also a little frustrated at my grandmother for putting me in the position she had. This was not a conversation that should have been taking place in a restaurant in front of my father, uncle, and brother. I tried to find a tactful way to handle it regardless of how I felt in the moment.

"Alright, Grandmother, I'll take a look when I get back to the Hollow and arrange for an interview this afternoon or tomorrow morning if she is interested."

"No, Paige, you misunderstand me. I don't want you to interview her, I want you to offer her a job, same as the other candidates you will be calling later this afternoon." Grandma Jane said

"Mom, you can't just hire this girl without at least having Paige talk to her first. You don't know anything about her or how she works, what skills she has, nothing," my Uncle Derrick chimed in, sensing the discomfort in the conversation.

"I absolutely can. If she turns out to be a terrible fit, Paige has the right to let her go, and you can all tell me how wrong I was." My grandmother was not making these statements in a fashion that garnered the option for much discussion. And yet, a discussion was definitely needed.

While she did indeed have the right to force my hand in this matter, it was not how we had operated for any decision up through this point, and I was not prepared to let it be how we moved forward.

"Grandma, I understand what you have hired me to do, and I know that part of my responsibility is ensuring we have the correct staff for our team. While that may include letting someone go in the future if they are not performing to our standard, it also includes making sound hiring decisions to hopefully avoid the former wherever possible. I am not comfortable extending the offer to this woman, sight unseen, without any information or references."

"Besides, if she did end up having to let her go," my father started, always the negotiator of the family, "what would your friend Sophia think? It would undoubtedly put a strain on your friendship."

"I promise to keep in mind that she is a family friend and will do everything I can to speak to her immediately, but I owe it to the other team members, and you, to do this process correctly. And if she is the right person for the team, I owe it to her as well. No one wants to feel like they were given a job out of pity and not because they were wanted for the role," I finished, being sure to be respectful in my tone, but also doing my best to garner an air of authority. After all, that is precisely why my grandmother hired me. She knew I wouldn't be a pushover. That included my interactions with her.

We could all see that she was not pleased by the fact that both my uncle and my father were in agreement with me. Ben wisely did not contribute to the conversation, but he did give me a subtle nod, letting me know he agreed with what I was saying as well.

"I appreciate that you are all willing to inform me how you think I should run this business, as well as what you think the right thing to do is. However, I have already informed Sophie that the job offer will be made. She called her granddaughter while I was there yesterday afternoon and told her the news. She is simply waiting to hear from you Paige, to finalize the agreement and paperwork."

Well then. That was that. I took a deep breath and said no more, since anything that would come out of my mouth was going to be neither respectful nor productive. I made the silent decision to bring her in anyways and get to know her first. If she was a terrible fit, maybe she'd listen to more reason than my grandmother seemed to be willing to do. If she decided to discipline me for the decision after the fact, so be it. I was determined to keep an open mind, even while my grandmother was tying my hands.

I picked up the envelope and opened it to see who the latest hire-apparent was. There was a piece of paper that contained her name, address, phone number, and a photo. When I was done studying the picture, I returned to the name written at the top. I couldn't help it, I started laughing... but in a crazy lady sort of way, not in a fun vacation sort of way. Maria Tomlinson. That was her name. Maria the Third. Unbelievable.

I needed this day to end.

CHAPTER ELEVEN

It's Beginning to Look a Lot Like Christmas

I left the restaurant and headed back to the inn. I could see Ben's truck behind me, so I knew he was following me there. My dad, uncle, and grandmother headed back home. I took the longer way back to the inn, needing a few minutes to myself before getting back to work. I still had a few things I needed to check on for the Christmas Eve extravaganza, but I'd have to do that once I finished up the afternoon's interviews. Just as well, I thought to myself, since I'd rather have the evening to myself.

Ben pulled up beside me when we did finally make it back to the Hollow, and waited for me as I gathered my things and locked up my car. "Paige," he started, unsure of what to say. I just shook my head.

"I know, Ben. I can't do it though. I am going to bring her in for an interview. I'll tell her it's a minor formality, but I cannot just offer her the job without at least meeting her and knowing more about her capabilities. It just doesn't feel right. If Grandma gets mad at me, so be it. At least I'll know I did the right thing."

"I'm proud of you," he said simply, giving me a hug.

"Thank you," I mumbled into his shoulder while my face was smooshed into it. I pulled away and we headed to the front door. "So, what brings you to the Hollow, aside from making sure I'm okay?"

"Jake asked me to double check a couple measurements for the decking of the halls that will take place tomorrow. He's also added to the to do list: test the surround sound to make sure music can be played in the main rooms. He knew I was meeting you all for lunch so he thought I might be able to do it on the way back to the office."

"Well then, don't let me hold you up. I'm going to attempt to reach Maria before my next interview arrives. Hey," I said turning to him as he headed toward the library and seating area. "Are you coming for the decking of the halls tomorrow? If you are, you and Jake can join me for the chef auditions. An extra couple of opinions might come in handy."

"Food? We'll be there. Are you conducting the auditions by yourself?"

"Well... not if you and Jake join me, but trying to hold them and make sure that the inn gets decorated appropriately is making it difficult to have anyone else come with me. Emily has conducted the phone interviews and checked references. My former boss and mentor, Jennifer, has also weighed in, so we're down to the final two with a heavy lean in one direction. I'm hoping that this next portion just solidifies what we've already mostly decided."

"You're not going to tell us which way you're leaning, are you?" Ben asked.

"I am not. I cannot add prejudice to the judges' table," I said smiling and waving as I headed into my little office under the stairs.

It was almost 5:00 by the time I wrapped up the last of the interviews. Maria was able to come in, and I actually felt much better about offering her a job once we talked. There were definitely things that she was going to have to learn, but she was grateful for the chance, had a sunny disposition, and seemed to be an incredibly hard worker. She brought with her several references for me to follow up on, and let me know that she was relieved when I told her I wanted to meet. She didn't feel one hundred percent right about just accepting the job because of who her grandmother was.

I knew I had to make several stops before my workday ended, but I wanted a few minutes to decompress, so I headed into the library, which was coming together splendidly. The fresh paint looked amazing, and the artwork and bookshelves that had been installed gave a formal but cozy feeling to the room. I sat on the floor—

folding my legs crisscross-applesauce—and started pulling books out of the three boxes that were filled to the brim. The furniture itself was going to be delivered the day after next, so I wanted to get as much accomplished before then as possible. It also meant that we could decorate the bookshelves for Christmas if we wanted to since the books would already have found their new homes.

My phone began vibrating on the floor next to me, and I looked over to check who was calling. It was Emily's sister, Heidi.

"Hello?" I asked when I answered the phone.

"Hi. I'm having a crisis of mental proportions," Heidi said dramatically. I smiled.

"Oh, dear. That does sound serious. What is the crisis and how can I help?"

"You can finish my dissertation for me. Or if that feels unacceptable, you can let me come out and hang with you and Emily this weekend before I lose my mind." Heidi was finishing up her doctorate and she had been working herself ragged for a while.

"I cannot promise we're going to be any fun whatsoever, but you know you never even need to ask. As for the writing of the dissertation, I will absolutely not be providing you that service. But I will buy you a treat to make you feel better about the work you still have."

"Deal. I'll see you this weekend!"

"Call your sister and let her know too," I said.

"Already did. She's working so she couldn't talk, but I left her a voicemail. Bye!"

"Bye!"

When I finished the books, I sent a quick text to both my parents and let them know I'd be late and not to wait on dinner for me. I triple checked my calendar for the next day to make sure that I had everything that needed to get done on the list. Between the chef auditions, decorating, and calls to make the offers for the positions we were filling, I was doing quite the time tango. I locked up the inn and then headed to finish the errands I hadn't been able to do earlier in the day.

First stop... the local Christmas tree lot. Ben and Jake were picking up the large tree for the main floor, but I wanted to do something special for all the guests, so I decided that I wanted to get small trees for each of the rooms. Instead of attempting to find the trees myself, I spoke to the lot owner and let him know what I was trying to do. He said he'd chat with Ben the following day when I sent them over, and he'd have all the trees delivered the following evening. I tried to pre-pay, but he was excited to have the business and was hoping that we could form an annual relationship, so he let me know he'd be happy to send an invoice along with the trees once they were delivered. He also said he wanted to make sure I got a fair price since I was buying in bulk. Until the inn, I didn't know that buying Christmas trees in bulk was even a thing.

Once the trees were taken care of, I headed to the craft store to pick up the list of the supplies I needed for the homemade Christmas stockings I would be decorating the banister with. Santa would obviously be making a visit to the inn, and he'd need stockings so that he could stuff them. I also found some ornament packs that I could use to decorate each of the guest room trees with.

Next stop was to Target to get... well everything else. By the time I finished there, it was almost 9:00, Phoebe could hold nothing more, and I was exhausted and hungry. I mentally waved the white flag of surrender, plopped myself into my car and headed home. There was still a lot to do, but I was going to be able to cross a lot of things off the to-do list the following morning.

The following morning, my alarm sounded far too early for my liking. I did not get enough sleep the night before because I was unable to turn off my brain when I needed to. I was hoping very much that Jake would bring the largest and strongest coffee he could find. In the meantime, I showered, applied the minimum amount of makeup necessary to keep me looking like an alive and functioning human being, threw on my comfiest pair of jeans, and a sweatshirt. I pulled back my hair into a messy bun at the top of my head, slid my feet into a pair of Uggs, and was out the door before I had time to reason myself out of it.

I was the first one at the inn, so I used the alone time to get myself organized for the rest of the day. I made a detailed timeline that included every single thing I could think of to ensure I knew where to be, and when. It was going to be another long day. I heard the front door open, and a familiar Christmas carol being whistled which let me know Jake had arrived.

"Good morning! Is anyone in the mood for some coffee and a cranberry scone?" He called as he closed the door behind him. I stepped out of the office under the stairs with my hand raised.

"Me! I'm in the mood for both of those things," I said.

He chuckled and then handed me both a large cup and a small white pastry bag. I closed my eyes and took a sip of the coffee and let out a contented sight. It was strong and hot, and he'd added milk and honey, my favorite. "Bless you, Jacob Kinnison. You are a Godsend."

"Did I get it right?" he asked, nodding towards the coffee cup.

"It is perfect." I took another sip and followed him towards the kitchen. Jake leaned up against the island while I hopped up on the counter across from him. We didn't have chairs yet, and I was still not awake enough to just stand. I took a bite of my cranberry scone and was once again grateful for Jake's existence. He popped open another pastry bag and took a bite out of something I couldn't quite make out.

"So, what's the plan for today?" he asked, taking another bite before he realized I had stopped eating my scone and was eyeing the pastry bag. "What?" he asked.

"What is that?" I said pointing to his breakfast treat. I was one of those people who had to know what everyone else was eating so that I could either be even more content with my choice, or be envious of theirs.

"A chocolate croissant," he said squinting his eyes at me. "I might be open to a barter, but there will be no trade."

I took another small bite of my cranberry scone to determine the price I was willing to pay for my second most favorite treat. I decided the scone was exactly what I needed it to be and opted to stick with my original option. "No thank you, I do not believe a barter is necessary today."

"But... what if I wanted some cranberry scone?" he asked, pretending to be offended.

"You don't. Trust me, you wouldn't like it at all. They're terrible."

"You are not a very good fibber," he said, laughing and taking another bite of his croissant.

"Thank you," I said as I pretended to curtsy from my perched position. "Now, back to work. I made a schedule," I said, nudging the notebook that was sitting next to me towards him a little, without getting scone bits on the paper. He crossed from the island to the counter and looked it over.

"This is very impressive. And also very busy. How are you going to get all of this done in a single day, exactly?" Jake said looking over at me. His face was very close to mine now and I couldn't help but have a hitch in my breath. Focus, Paige. I turned to set my scone down and picked up my coffee cup to give me a minute to gather myself.

"I will not be getting all of this done. Surprise! See here, the different colors? Those represent you, me, and Ben."

"So, you're pink, I'm..." he studied the list for a minute before finishing, "green, and Ben's red? Got it. But it's still mostly pink, for the record."

"Yes, but I have a lot of littler things. Like all the calls I have to make, that's like fifteen lines alone. I can do all of that while you and Ben are hanging the Christmas lights."

"Understood. Well, according to this you're five minutes late and I was hoping you might be willing to help me unload the truck, so really you're further behind than that," he said.

"I'm willing to help unload yours, if you're willing to help unload mine. Deal?" I said, sticking my hand out so we could shake on it.

"Deal," he said, shaking my hand and then grabbing the list off the counter while I hopped down. "We should get started. Don't forget your coffee, you're going to need it today."

We got both cars unloaded and Jake got to work on Operation Deck the Halls while I started making the calls for the job offers. Ben arrived a little while later and before long it was time for the first chef auction. I had the two men wash up and head to the kitchen as I welcomed Sharon to the inn.

Sharon had started culinary school in New York City, but ended up returning home after a few semesters in order to help take care of her mother, who had broken a hip and needed help. Her audition went well. She made us several different kinds of eggs, some French toast, and a berry parfait. She also handed each of us copies of a calendar with menu items for each meal on it. She thanked us for our time and was on her way quicker than I would have thought possible, the kitchen sparkling and clean as though she'd never been there at all.

When she had driven away, I called Jennifer and put her on speaker phone so that we could walk her through what had just happened. I had asked all the questions she'd given me, but I still wanted to make sure Ben, Jake, and I knew what we were looking for. We each reviewed our notes with Jennifer about both the food and the interview questions. Before giving us any feedback, Jennifer asked what we thought of her overall.

"I liked her," I said. Ben agreed and Jake added that the food was delicious, but that he didn't really feel like he could give an opinion on the other things. I got up and grabbed each of us a bottle of water out of the fridge, and then Jennifer started to give us feedback based on what she'd heard us say.

"Keep in mind, I didn't meet her myself, nor have I tasted her food, but from what I am hearing each of you say, her food was good. I would have liked her to have brought a list of ingredients or asked about special dietary needs, as well as go into detail about how the food was prepped and prepared. It does seem like she has some schooling, but it also sounds like she's been away from the business for a little while, which makes sense based on what she told you before the audition started," Jennifer said.

"So... we don't like her?" Jake asked.

I laughed. "I think we still like her, I just also think that we would like her more if she'd had some of that information. It'll be something we can look for in the other audition," I answered, picking up on what Jennifer was trying to say. It had been almost a year since I'd been involved with any auditions for the kitchen, but it was starting to come back to me.

"Exactly. Nothing that happened was a deal breaker by any means, and my guess is if you asked her, she'd be able to provide that information to you, even after the fact. So don't count her out yet. Let's see what happens with the next one. When is it?" Jennifer said.

Earlier, I'd made a copy of the schedule so that both Ben and Jake could also have one, and then I'd stuck the original in my folio that could go with me everywhere I went. I pulled it out and looked it over to get Jennifer the information she needed. "Looks like we have a couple of hours before the next one, which is good because I have to go pick up invitations and finish making phone calls," I said, the last part more to myself than anyone else.

"Perfect. Call me when the next one is complete and we can go from there," Jennifer said. We all thanked her before signing off.

"Alright, we need to get back out there and finish those lights so that you can call the Christmas tree man and get that all sorted," Jake said, patting Ben on the back.

"Yes, the trees! I cannot wait for those to get here," I said, standing up. I headed back to the office under the stairs and grabbed my purse and my car keys and then headed outside to the porch where Ben and Jake were getting back to hanging the rest of the Christmas lights. It was cold outside, and the air was adding to the feeling of Christmas. I was excited. "You two be safe! I'll be back soon," I hollered as I climbed in my car and backed out of the parking lot.

A couple of days earlier, Ben had mentioned that Jake didn't have any plans for Christmas Eve. He was going to see his parents on Christmas Day, but they had a party or something they were going to the night before. I asked him if he thought it would be weird if I invited Jake to join us for the festivities on Christmas Eve. He wouldn't be staying at the inn obviously, but at least he could enjoy the amazing things Emily and I had planned for the evening. Ben thought it was a great idea. Coincidentally, so did my sister, so I made her swear that she would not attempt any further matchmaking meddling. Jake didn't know it yet, but there would be a stocking with his name on it, as well as a beautifully hand printed invitation upon my return.

Dolores was in the shop when I arrived, and she proudly presented me with the invitations. They were absolutely beautiful. I was so excited to be sending them out the following day. I also had a chance to talk with her about some of the other items that I thought could be great for the inn and she said she could have samples for me just before the new year. I thanked her again and wished her a very Merry Christmas.

By the time I got back to the inn, Ben and Jake were busy decorating the porch railings with garland. I could see a small stack of wreaths sitting on one of the porch chairs that I was excited to see hung up. I had only known of the large one that was going on the front door, so clearly the men had something else up their sleeves. Hummingbird Hollow was going to look absolutely amazing.

As I finished my final job offer, I heard Ben and Jake enter again and head towards the laundry area to wash up. Checking my clock, I saw that it was time for the final chef audition. I quickly pulled out the stockings and felt paint that I would use to put names on them, so that I was already set up for my next to-do when we wrapped up this interview.

From the onset, the second audition felt entirely different than the first. The chef's name was Alice and when we greeted her at the front door, she had three people behind her carrying serving trays. One of the trays had three champagne flutes on it. Each flute was filled with what looked like Christmas in a glass. It turned out to be sparkling apple cider, with several cranberries and a sprig of sugared rosemary. It was simple, but beautiful. Before we were each handed a glass, Alice asked if we had any dietary restrictions or allergies that she should be aware of. One point for Alice! We each said no and were rewarded with the tasty beverages.

"If you would, please follow me," Alice said, heading toward the dining room area. I could tell by the looks on their faces that Ben and Jake were befuddled on how she could possibly know where to go, but I knew from the video interview that I'd already had with her that she'd asked for a tour of the main floor and the kitchen area to get a feel for the inn.

When we got to the dining room area, Alice quickly pointed to one of the tables, and the three assistants headed over and started setting up. Alice pulled off her messenger bag and set it down next to her. She then reached out and shook each of our hands. "I know formal introductions are usually how these things start, but I like to let my food speak for itself. Also, just between us, I don't tend to be an overly formal person, so this way we all can feel comfortable. In this business, relationships are as important as the food, and I want us to feel like family," she finished before heading over to the table and making sure the food was being set up to her liking.

I felt a nudge on my arm and turned to look at Jake as he wiggled his eyebrows at me, letting me know he was impressed. I couldn't help it, I quietly giggled. Ben also gave me a thumbs up and took another sip of his mocktail.

Alice turned back to us and welcomed us to a beautifully set table. The assistants, who were now moving to the back of the room and doing their best to be invisible, had covered the table in a beautiful dark emerald green tablecloth, set down gold chargers—the fancy little plates that go under the real plates—and garnet colored cloth napkins. "Please, have a seat and we'll get started," Alice said, smiling and then quickly turning to her entourage and thanking them for a job well done. I made a mental note because regular praise for a job well done—even when it was a small thing—was a big part of how I liked to treat my staff as well.

I hadn't noticed it before, but sitting in front of each of us was a small menu listing the items that we would be tasting. The tiny tasting menu had been carefully crafted, the lettering and artwork lending further to the Christmas theme of the tablescape. I, for one, appreciated the attention to detail. Alice gestured to her team and they brought the first plate over. She took the time to describe what we were eating, how it had been prepared, and also spoke briefly about alternative options that could be made available for patrons that did have dietary restrictions in order to allow them to enjoy similar flavors and textures. Each subsequent course followed in the same fashion.

Throughout the meal, it was clear that Alice not only enjoyed what she did, but had a tremendous knowledge of food, ingredients, and different ways of preparing dishes.

She also made it obvious through her dishes that she believed there was a time to play it safe with food, and a time to experiment and take risks. Both, she explained, were vital in creating menus that people enjoyed and did not tire of.

When we reached the end of the meal, Alice gestured to each of her assistants, each of whom she had made sure to introduce to us during the various courses. Sasha walked over and quickly cleared the last of the small plates away, resetting the dessert tableware to the right and the left of the setting, and removing the remaining unused silverware from the original setup. Next, Taylor brought over a tray holding three martini glasses that had some sort of dessert in them, while Marcus brought over a small carafe that contained coffee, offering each of us a cup.

"I did a little research and learned that you love strawberries and dark chocolate," Alice said, gesturing toward the martini glasses. "So, for dessert today, we have a cheesecake parfait with chocolate covered strawberries. It is absolutely divine, if I do say so myself," she said laughing. I lifted my spoon to the glass. It was amazing. It was like she had somehow taken all of the best parts of cheesecake, and none of the annoying parts, and made it into the perfect dessert. "This might be the best dessert I've ever had in my life," Ben said, putting words to what I had only been thinking.

Next, Alice went to her messenger bag and pulled out three small binders. She handed one to each of us. "I took the liberty of making a sample menu for a month. You'll notice that each day has two alternatives listed just in case something unexpected were to come up, like certain fruits or vegetables not being available or something. Also included are my references, a sample rotation schedule for my team, and finally, in the very back of the binder are the three sample menus for Christmas Eve and Christmas morning. You will see my interpretation of your traditional family meals. The four of us will be available on Christmas Eve to ensure that everything you need is ready. I can also be available on Christmas morning if you need me to come in and get anything setup for you, but my team will have the day off, and I would need to be off by ten in the morning so that I can spend the day with my family."

Alice had mentioned on the phone that she had three team members that would be who she expected to hire if she got the job, and that we could discuss the other positions that would need to be filled at a later time. The gesture of being available for the holiday on such short notice was very touching and entirely unexpected. We finished up the rest of the interview and said our goodbyes, but I knew even before Jennifer picked up her phone that Alice McDaniels was going to be the new chef for Hummingbird Hollow.

I also knew which of the menus my family was going to be enjoying on Christmas Eve.

CHAPTER TWELVE

T-Minus Three Days and Counting

It was Monday morning, December twenty-first. Ben had let me know after the audition with Alice the Friday earlier that the Christmas trees were not going to be delivered until Monday morning because the owner needed to wait for a second truckload from his farm to get the appropriate number of smaller trees for the guest rooms. Jake offered to be there first thing in the morning to meet the delivery guys, if I promised to be the coffee runner for the day. So, color me surprised when my phone started ringing at seven thirty in the morning while I was still in my jammies and the caller ID read 'Jake'.

"Paige, how close are you to getting down here?" he asked without so much as a greeting. That could not have been a good sign.

"Umm, I was finishing up with some of the last-minute touches for Christmas Eve and then planning on hopping in the shower... so maybe like an hour? Why, what's wrong?"

"Any chance you can shave that time a little? There is an issue with the trees, and I don't want to make a call on your behalf."

"What's wrong with the delivery? Like we don't have enough, they're the wrong size?" I asked, starting to panic a little. It must have been pretty bad if Jake didn't want to make a decision on it.

"It's kind of hard to explain over the phone. Just get here when you can. In the meantime, Ben is on his way so maybe he can help until you get here."

"Alright, I'll be there soon," I said, hanging up and running to the bathroom to get the shower started so the water could heat up. I then headed back to my room and took everything I had been working on and tossed it into my bag. I'd just have to finish up at the inn once I got the whole mystery tree debacle sorted out.

My dad was in the hallway watching the orchestrated chaos, and by the time I was out of the shower and dressed, he was leaning on the bathroom doorframe while I brushed my wet hair and tossed it into a low bun. "What's the rush, hon? It's cold out there, and wet hair is only going to make it worse," Dad said.

"I know, but I have to get to the inn. Jake is there and there has been some sort of giant mess up with the..." I caught myself before I slipped up and blabbed about the trees, "a delivery. Jake and Ben are trying to get it sorted but they said they need me there."

"Anything I can do to help?" he asked, as I shut off the bathroom light, headed back into my room and grabbed my coat and my bag and then searched for a minute for my phone and my car keys.

"I don't think so, but I'll let you know if that changes," I said, kissing him on the cheek and then running down the stairs.

"Drive carefully please! I love you," he called after me.

"Love you too!" I hollered heading into the garage and firing Phoebe up. I didn't care how late I was, coffee was a necessity, and the crisis was just going to have to hold off a little bit longer. I opened up my phone and called my favorite coffee shop, placing a phone order for myself, Jake, and Ben so that it would be ready by the time I got there, and then pulled out of the garage.

By the time I arrived at the inn, I could see Ben and Jake's trucks in the parking lot, but no truck with trees. That could not be a good sign, I thought to myself as I parked. As I tried to gather everything that needed to make it into the main house without spilling the coffee, Jake came out to meet me. "Where is the Christmas tree man?" I said, as he took the coffee tray from me, as well as the bags I had in my hand.

"I had nothing to do with this," Ben called from the porch where he stood waiting. I was confused, so I looked to Jake for clarification.

"Okay, please don't be mad," Jake said, smiling at me innocently. I stopped in my tracks.

"Jake, you are really starting to freak me out,"

"There is no emergency..." he said, before standing and blocking my way in case I decided to storm away dramatically, which I might have done had I not been so relieved to hear it. There wasn't any time left for emergencies.

"What do you mean?" I said, my voice abnormally calm even though my heart rate hadn't quite gotten the message yet.

"Come inside and let me show you," he said, heading towards where Ben stood waiting to relieve him of all the items that he had taken from me. Once Jake's hands were free, he took mine. "I'm sorry for making you worry but I couldn't stand it any longer. Trust me?" It was a question, not a statement.

"Not at the moment really," I said honestly. Ben snickered.

"That's fair. Would you please close your eyes anyways?" Jake said. I did as he asked, and he led me into the foyer before letting go of my hands. "Okay, open them."

I did, and I couldn't believe my eyes. Hummingbird Hollow was dressed to the nines for Christmas. All of the furniture pieces that I thought weren't coming yet were in place. Everything was finished. Ben—who had taken all of my stuff to the office under the stairs, bringing back the coffees and pastry bags and setting them on the front desk—joined us then. Wordlessly they led me to the library and sitting room where the Christmas tree—which was beautifully decorated—shone brightly next to a lit fire. It was magical.

"You two did all this?" I asked, continuing to look around in awe.

"We thought it was only fair you get a surprise for Christmas too. Come upstairs and let us show you the bedrooms. We think we got the tree themes right for each of them," Jake said as Ben led the way. We did a complete tour of the main house, and I couldn't believe my eyes. Everything looked better than I could have ever imagined. I couldn't help it, I started to tear up at it. I hoped my grandmother would be proud. I knew Laurie would have been.

By the time the tour was finished, I was not only not even the slightest bit upset at the trick, I was beyond grateful for both Ben and for Jake. We grabbed our coffee and our pastries, and we headed into the sitting area and made ourselves cozy while we had our breakfast and chatted. Jake officially accepted his invitation to Christmas Eve at Hummingbird Hollow, even more grateful to know that it hadn't been rescinded based on his lousy prank.

When we were done eating, we turned off the fireplace, and both Jake and Ben headed out to wrap up their remaining work before the holiday break. I headed back into my office, heart full of gratitude and renewed energy to make sure Christmas Eve was the best it could be. Ben had turned on instrumental Christmas music through the central speakers on the main floor, and I realized he and Jake had made sure one of the speakers made it into the office area so that I too could enjoy the music, which I did while I got down to work.

First, I called my dad and let him know that everything at the inn was taken care of and that he didn't need to worry about anything. He asked if he, Emily, and Heidi could meet me at the inn for lunch. Trying to keep everyone away from the property for the final days was getting harder to do, but thankfully David was scheduled to finish up the pool area and gardens through the twenty-third, so I had a ready excuse. Instead, I suggested we meet at the house, and I'd pick something up on my way back. If I worked from home for the afternoon, it was less likely anyone would be tempted to head to me. Besides, Emily and I had some secret conversations that needed to take place about the schedule of events on the twenty-fourth.

When I finished on the phone with him, I called Alice and made an official offer, completing my employee roster. Alice asked if we could meet at the inn the following day to finalize the Christmas menus, as well as the plans she had for tablescapes. Once that plan was set, I headed upstairs to put some finishing touches in each of the guest rooms.

My mom texted the whole family letting us know that Grandma Rose was making everyone dinner because my aunt and uncle were getting back in town that night. She wanted to make sure we arrived by 5:30. I sent back a thumbs up, knowing that it would be easier to be on time since I'd be coming from the house with my dad and Em.

By the time I was ready to pick up lunch and head home for the day, I couldn't wait for Christmas Eve to arrive.

When I got to the inn the following day, I spent the first part of the morning getting a tour of the work that David had done. The gardens were magnificent. So was the outside entertainment area. I made a mental note to show Alice that space when she arrived a little later that morning. When David's tour was complete, I headed to the office and grabbed the camera I'd remembered to bring from home. I wanted to make sure I took photos of all of the rooms so that we could have a historical record of how Hummingbird Hollow had started. I had been doing it at every major stage of the renovation. It seemed only fitting to be doing it at the end.

Alice arrived while I was in the final guest room. I heard her calling out, and let her know I was upstairs and would be down in a moment. I met her at the front desk, where she promptly handed me a cup that matched the one in her hand.

"Good morning," she said smiling. "I tried to make as much noise as possible as I came in. I am always so in the zone when I'm working that someone could come right up behind me and I wouldn't ever even realize they were there until they tapped me on the shoulder. Usually scares the pants right off me!"

I smiled back at her and took a sip of the hot beverage she'd handed me. It was clearly peppermint cocoa, only better somehow. It tasted like Christmas in a cup. She smiled when she saw the look of surprise and delight on my face.

"It's good right? It was my grandma's secret recipe. Though, I might have tweaked it a little," she said.

"Thank you, Alice, this was so sweet of you, and it is absolutely amazing. I know we have a lot to talk about, but I was wondering if you would like an official tour of the property before we get into all that stuff."

"I'd absolutely love that," she said. We spent the next forty-five minutes walking the entire property from tip to tail. "This place is absolutely amazing," she said when we finished the main house. "Your family is going to be so amazed at what you've done here. I cannot wait to hear their reactions to the surprise!"

"Wait until you see the surprises I have for you outside," I said laughing. I showed her the outdoor entertainment space, complete with a small, but fully functioning kitchen unit. I also took her down to the pool deck and the grassy knoll that could be great for picnics. Finally, I took her to the space where David had built beautiful raised beds for a garden. I told her the things that he was ready to plant for her, as well as the fact that he'd be by a little later on in the day if she had any special requests. She decided she'd wait for him and they could talk and figure out how to make her vision come to life. "I've always wanted a garden that I could use to inspire recipes," she said looking around the space. "This is going to be perfect."

By the time we headed back into the main house, I already felt like Alice and I were going to become great friends. We headed into the dining room so that we could get down to brass tacks about the food portion of the holiday. I had let Alice know on the phone the day before which menu I thought sounded most like the Italian

Christmas feasts we'd had as a family for as long as I could remember.

"I know you always have Italian sausage grinders and pasta con agile e olio d'olivo for your main course, so I want to honor that. I did think it could be fun to add a couple of different spins on it. Nothing too crazy of course, just something to freshen up the tradition. I have added an enhanced topping bar for the sausages, as well as stepped up the rolls to be homemade. I also added my own personal cheese blend that I think will go great. As for the olive oil, since that is going to be the main sauce for the pasta, I thought it could be fun to play with that a little too. You mentioned that often times you have to split the servings, so that some have plain garlic and olive oil, and some have anchovies. I have a little bit of a superpower when it comes to infusing oils, and I was just wondering if you would give me a little leeway with that particular piece of the meal..." Alice said, looking at me with an anxious grimace.

"Yes," I said with more authority than I felt at the moment. I knew messing with our traditions was something we hadn't done and people like my sister held them very close to the heart, but I hadn't had anything that Alice had made that was bad, and the Hollow's kitchen was now hers. Frankly I had no doubt that she would do my family proud.

"Are you sure, Paige? I don't want to just go butting my nose into a family tradition," she said.

"I'm sure. I trust you. Besides, one of the things I'm learning from this entire experience, is that it is not a bad thing to stir up the water every now and again. I'm excited to see what you do with it," I said, realizing that I meant every word.

Next, we moved on to Christmas morning and the items she'd have prepared for easy heat-and-eat. She also asked about Christmas dinner, but my Grandma Rose had that covered with homemade gnocchi and meatballs. I was going to head over to the house on Christmas Eve morning and pick up everything my grandmother would need for us to make the meal at the inn. She asked if I wanted her to be at the inn Christmas morning to help out, but I let her know that I wanted her to be at home spending the day with her family. She was due to go to her parents' house in the afternoon but was willing to come by on the way. I told her thank you, but no. She'd already given up her Christmas Eve for us, I wouldn't have her giving up her Christmas Day.

"Are you kidding me? I cannot wait to be a fly on the wall when your family gets here! Christmas Eve is going to be a blast!"

Finally, we spoke about tablescapes and what her vision was for Christmas Eve. She also insisted on prepping the dining room for Christmas dinner, since Christmas morning would be served buffet style directly in the kitchen and eaten around the Christmas tree while presents were being opened.

By the time Alice left, there was nothing else to plan for food, and I—for one—was getting hungry even thinking about it. I headed upstairs and finished the decorating, since when I left the inn that night, I wouldn't be back until Christmas Eve. I had plans to help Grandma Jane finish her Christmas shopping and then had a date with myself to finish wrapping presents.

Ready or not, Christmas was just around the corner. Thanks to Ben, Jake, David, and Alice, I was feeling more ready than I ever thought I would.

CHAPTER THIRTEEN

Home is Where The Hearts Are

"Take a deep breath. Are you ready for this?" Emily asked, standing next to me behind the reception desk. She was wearing a gorgeous cream sweater and grey pants. We had both decided that we should be dressed up a little bit in order to welcome our very first guests. I hadn't told Emily about the biggest surprise of all, because I wanted her to be surprised along with everyone else. It had been incredibly difficult, but I'd kept her busy all morning with different tasks around the outside and main floor of the inn.

Now that my family was due to start arriving any minute, she had come back inside to help greet them. I was wearing a red turtleneck sweater with black slacks. My hair was pulled back into a neat low ponytail. Alice had been in the kitchen all morning, humming cheerily along to the Christmas music being piped in through the amazing sound system. It was quickly becoming one of my favorite features of the inn. Now, she came out to join us in greeting everyone as they arrived.

Late Tuesday afternoon I had received a couple of voicemails from two of the valets, Steve and Ryan, letting me know they wanted to come in and help make sure everyone had their cars parked for them and their luggage carried to their rooms. Apparently, the new staff was as excited as I was to be opening the doors to our first guests, even if they were my family. I agreed to allow them to come in only after I made them promise to be home before their own Christmas Eve festivities began with their families.

Steve and Ryan were standing in the foyer next to Alice, who was bouncing excitedly with the anticipation of the arrival of our first group.

"I cannot believe we did this," I said to Emily, finally answering her question after a long pause.

"It's going to be great, you know," she said leaning into me and giving me a happy little nudge.

I finally took the deep breath she had asked me to take a few minutes earlier. "I really hope so, Em. I'm really proud of this place and what everyone has done. And the truth is, even Grandma Jane hasn't seen most of the little details we've put into it..."

All of the sudden, we heard the first two cars pulling up the driveway. "I'll get the cars, if you want to do the luggage," Steve said to Ryan, coming up with a plan without being asked. Ryan nodded in agreement and positioned himself off to the side of the reception desk.

"It's show time!" Alice said as we saw the cars come into view. Steve headed quickly out the front door and down to the half-moon driveway where the cars—a red Toyota Prius and a Chevy Silverado—pulled up and parked.

It was my parents and Jake. I smiled. There was no one I was happier about having here first than my mom and dad.

Everything was always less scary with them there, no matter how old I got. I watched as my parents climbed out of the car and then watched as three more people started climbing out of the backseat. That meant Grandma Jane, Uncle Derrick, and Aunt Charlotte were also here. Before they finished unloading their luggage, Jake said a quick word to Steve and then pulled around the Prius and parked his truck next to mine. Since he didn't have any luggage, he wasn't going to need Ryan's services. I watched him as he headed around the side and came through the kitchen.

"Ryan, why don't you head out and get their bags? Between Emily, Alice and myself—" I started, but was interrupted by Jake's sudden appearance by Alice's side.

"And me. Hi," he said waving and smiling at all of us. "Sorry I was just thinking I could also be put to work,"

I nodded my thanks before continuing. "Ahem, between Emily, Alice, Jake and I, we'll be able to get them to their rooms without any trouble," I finished smiling and giving him a little nod.

As Ryan headed out to get the bags, Jake squeezed Alice's arm in greeting before heading over to me and whispering, "You really did it. Hummingbird Hollow Inn is officially open for business." He smiled at me with a look of pride. "Also… you look beautiful, by the way." I couldn't help it, I felt both compliments all the way down to my toes.

Before I could thank him and remind him that none of it would have been possible without his help, Emily became all business. "Alright, which room are they in?" she asked. Unable to resist, I let out a tiny squeal and then smooshed her into a giant hug. The truth was, while there were plenty of days that we were ready to strangle each other, none of that mattered in the long run. It was what made our friendship so amazing. There was no one that I would rather succeed, or fail, with than my best friend. Watching Emily kick into high gear for my family… our family, I was once again reminded of how lucky I was to have her. That was right before she pushed me away. "Alright, alright, I love you too now get off me. You'll muss me," she said.

She went back to pulling up the reservations so that she could have the keys ready in the few seconds it would take before everyone walked in. I felt it the moment she tensed up and started to panic. "Paige! These rooms are not numbered in the system like they should be! Something is totally wrong! You'll need to find a way to stall them until I can figure it out…" I watched the panic grow on her face as she continued to try to scroll through the computer. She was at war with herself mentally, trying to keep me from panicking and also trying to wrack her brain for a way to fix the problem in the two point five seconds we had until my parents, grandmother, aunt and uncle all reached the front desk.

I put my hand over hers and made her stop moving. "Emily, stop. Nothing is broken I promise."

"Well, it cannot be fine because there are no freaking room numbers for our guest rooms. How can we assign rooms to our guests if we do not know which ones are available because they aren't numbered?"

"Your turn. Take a deep breath. I didn't number them. It's not a mistake." It was time to let Emily in on the final secret that Hummingbird Hollow had to offer. Thankfully, my parents entered, allowing me to reveal it to everyone at once. I gently nudged Emily to the side, taking position in front of the computer, and turned my attention to our latest arrivals.

"Merry Christmas! Welcome to Hummingbird Hollow. My name is Paige, and I will be checking you in this evening. This is Alice, the inn's head chef, and Emily one of the managers here," I said, smiling brightly. "And this is Jake and he is..." I faltered for a moment, unsure of how to introduce him.

"Handyman extraordinaire," Jake added waving to everyone and winking at me. I returned my attention to the group standing in front of me. I wanted the family to get the same treatment the rest of our guests would.

"Yes, we're here and checking in. Last name, Donovan," my dad said, playing along. He gave me a little wink as well.

Emily continued to smile brightly as she whispered to Jake and I, "I'd love to look up their reservation for them but somebody played with the system without asking and now I don't know what the heck I'm doing."

I cleared my throat and Alice took over, introducing herself and asking if everyone had an enjoyable trip and if there were any special requests on the food front while they were staying at the inn. I whispered back to Emily, "I did ask permission, it just wasn't to you. Bartender Bob is excellent at altering things for people with strange requests like me. Now relax and scootch and I'll show you."

I typed a couple of things into the computer and pulled up my parent's, aunt and uncle's, and grandmother's reservations. "Here we go. I have three rooms for Donovan. One for Charles, one for Derrick, and one for Jane. Is that correct?"

"Yes, it is," my grandmother said, getting into the spirit of things.

"Excellent. I have your room keys right here, and whenever you are ready, Ryan and... Jake will be able to take your bags and show you to your rooms." I smiled at Jake. If he wanted to help, I was going to let him help. I pulled out five keys that sat on metal key rings—we were an inn for goodness' sake; none of those impersonal plastic credit cards or mobile app keyless entry for us—and handed the first set to my father, the second set to my uncle, and the final key to my grandmother. They looked at the keys for a moment, or more specifically at the key rings, and then looked back at me. I just smiled and nodded.

My dad looked over to my grandmother's key ring and read hers, and then looked over at my uncle's to see if his was the same. My uncle was busy looking at my grandmother. She kept looking from the key ring to me. Emily leaned over the counter to try to get a look at the keys, but when that didn't work for her, she pulled open the drawer and grabbed the second key to my grandmother's room.

"Paige. Why is my key ring engraved with the name Jimmy on it?" Grandma Jane finally asked.

I took a deep breath, and below the counter, Jake squeezed my hand reassuringly. He and Ben loved the secret when I told them. Now it was time to tell everyone else. "Grandma, when you bought this place, you said it was for our family. To bring all of us together. To give us a legacy. So, I started to look at this place as the heart of our family, you know? Something that everyone had a hand in making. Then I started thinking that if the inn was like the heart, then the rooms are kind of like the rooms in our heart;

the places where we keep all the things that are most important to us."

Everyone was just looking at me. I started to lose my nerve, but Alice caught my eye, and she was smiling and gave me a wink of encouragement. I reached out and found Jake's hand and without thinking held it to help steady me. He didn't even flinch.

I continued.

"After doing a lot of research on other inns, I realized how easy it would be to make our rooms different. Anyone can number some doors. But I thought we should pay tribute to those family members who are here with us in spirit; who touch our lives each and every day and have been on this journey right alongside us." I shrugged. "So, I named the rooms instead of numbering them. Because they are a part of this place too; in some ways even more so than each of us. They're our foundation as much as we are, and this inn is their legacy." I smiled, growing more confident when I remembered why I made the decision I had. "Inside each of the rooms is a piece of who they were, and who we remember them to be. That way they get to be as permanent a part of this place as the rest of us."

"You named the rooms?" my dad asked again, in disbelief.

"After family members?" my mom said at almost the same time.

"I did. All fifteen rooms. Each room pays tribute to someone we love. Grandma Jane, you are staying in Jimmy's room in honor of Grandpa Jimmy. Uncle Derrick? You'll be staying in Helen's room in honor of Aunt Helen." I turned to my parents. "You two will be staying in Nonni's room."

Everyone was quiet for a moment, processing what I had just said. Finally, my uncle asked, "and the other rooms?"

"There is Elias' room where Uncle Simon and Aunt Charlotte will be staying. There is also Elva's room, Tony's room, and Angie's room where Grandma Rose and Grandpa Frank will be staying. Bernie's room for Uncle Robert, who will be staying there with Aunt Lynn. Billy's room after your father, Grandma. Then there's Jan's room, Kent's room, Johnny's room, John's room, and Laurie's room," I finished turning to Emily. "That's where you and Heidi will be staying tonight." I counted quickly in my head... I was missing one. "Oh, and lastly there's Bella's room."

"Bella's room?" my mom asked looking surprised.

"We've had a lot of pets in this family. Mostly dogs, some cats. They've all touched our hearts just as much as each person named. So, I dedicated one of the rooms to them. It's for all of them: Gypsy, Sasha, Gretchen, Bridgette, Mandy, Penny, Daisy, Rusty, Tigger, Charlotte, Bella, Maggie, Amy, Abby, Dickens, Oliver, Nicholas, Sophie, Bailey, Cinder, Lucy, Riley, Kyra... each and every one. I thought they should all be a part of this place as well."

Emily opened the drawer where the keys were kept once more. Each one had a different key ring engraved with the names of the rooms on it. "The doors have name plaques instead of numbers?" she asked. I smiled and nodded.

"Would you all like to see what she has done?" Alice asked. "Paige has added beautiful touches of each of your family members so that they all live on in this place. It's really special. I'll hold down the fort here so that she can take you." I smiled again at Alice. I was really glad she was there with us for that moment.

We all turned and headed upstairs to take a look. The first room we came to on the left was Jimmy's room. I opened the door for everyone and then stepped back. The bedding and the furniture were simply done. The fabrics were a deep blue color, and the furniture was dark cherry wood. On the nightstand was an alarm clock radio that looked like an old 1940s radio. It was playing Glen Miller softly in the background. There were a few books on a shelf, and next to it was a picture frame with a black and white photo of my grandma and grandpa on their wedding day. It had always been my absolute favorite photo of them. To the average guest staying at the inn, it would look like a prop, but to my family, it was their story. There was also a small desk with writing paper and pens, and next to it was a framed letter from WWII. It was a copy of one of the letters my grandpa had sent to my grandma while he was on tour. It was folded so that the message inside stayed private, but it made for a beautiful piece of art.

"This is amazing," my uncle said. "You did a great job, Paige. Your grandpa would be very proud."

"Look at the Christmas tree," my mom said, her eyes filled with tears.

"Mom, don't cry! Yes. I thought each room needed a little something special. You love Christmas trees," I said, walking over and linking my arm through hers.

"I do. I love Christmas trees, and I love these rooms. It's a really neat idea," she said. I looked at her again. "Shut up, I can cry if I want to!" she said, laughing and sticking her tongue out at me.

"Grandma?" I asked. She was the one I needed to love the idea. She was also the one who hadn't given any indication of what she was thinking.

"Your Grandpa Jimmy loved Glen Miller. He had a radio just like that one. It's like he's in the room with us…" she trailed off but smiled. She liked it.

"Ready to see some more?" I asked everyone as Jake placed Grandma's overnight bag on the luggage rack. We headed across the hall to the next door. The plaque on the door read 'NONNI'S ROOM' in beautiful scroll lettering.

I opened the door and stepped off to the side once more. Everyone joined me, and Ryan placed two bags next to a curio cabinet and quietly left the room. The room was decorated, not how I remembered my Grandma Nonni's room to be decorated, but rather inspired by the things that reminded me of her. The fabrics were rich in color and textures, making you feel almost like you could drink them in. There were beautiful pictures of Italian bottles filled with rich liquids like wine, olive oil and vinegar on the wall, as well as one with handmade baskets filled with flowers and peppers. When I thought of my great-grandmother, I always thought about her and wonderful food. She believed food was something to be savored. That real, simple, quality ingredients mattered. There was a large bowl of fresh fruit on the table in the room, and in one corner there was a black and white photograph of my great-grandmother holding one of the porcelain dolls my mom had bought for her birthday. She had a collection. My mom walked over and picked up the photograph.

"I didn't want to put the actual dolls in here, because I thought they could get a little creepy, but I wanted them to be represented somehow," I said to her. She didn't say anything back, she just nodded and squeezed my hand.

When we left Nonni's room we headed next door to where Emily would be staying. I handed her the key and let her open the door to Laurie's room. I wasn't exactly sure what type of reaction I would get for this one. Actually, that wasn't entirely true. I knew my mom would be crying for sure. What I didn't know was how Emily or Heidi would react. They were both pretty great at not showing emotion and I wasn't sure if Em was going to be mad if I made her cry in front of everyone, especially without any warning.

I took a deep breath as she opened the door and walked in. I had everyone enter the room before me. Aside from John's room, this was the most difficult for me to walk into, but once I was inside, both rooms really brought me a lot of comfort.

Emily was walking around the room taking everything in. The room was done in a light lavender color, with a beautiful quilt spread on the bed. I remembered how Laurie used to make quilts and give them to people she loved. She was always an artist and had so many modalities. I knew when I did this room, everything needed to be handmade and one of a kind, because if anything said Laurie Nettle it was beautiful, handcrafted, artistic, and creative.

The bookshelves had some books on knitting and jewelry making, and the art on the walls was colorful and bold. Emily walked into the bathroom, my favorite part of the entire room. I had done my best to replicate the design of Laurie's bathroom at home, only I'd added a claw-foot tub, something she'd talked about having one day. The shower itself was stone with touches of shells, beads, and sparkling pieces of mirror and glass, creating the overall feel of an underwater cove. I couldn't help but smile every single time I saw the bathroom.

"Well..." I started to ask, but then stopped, not quite sure how to continue. I looked over to my mom who was once again crying, but she was also smiling at the same time, which always made my favorite face. I couldn't help but smile back at her. I turned to Emily. Her eyes were moist, but she was smiling. She didn't say anything, but she nodded at me. That was enough. It was all I needed to know that she approved. I nodded back. "Well, let's go see the rest."

And we did. As we headed into each room, the little touches that I'd hoped would remind my family of their loved ones were pointed out as delightful surprises. Each room took on the personality not only of the one it was named after, but of those they were most important to. Kent's room was filled with handmade woodworking, nature, and images of him tinkering in his garage. Elva's room had a picture of sisters holding hands and walking together. Bernie's room had a shadow box with old Ford memorabilia in it. Bella's room had artwork of the animals that had once been ours.

The final room was John's room. Most of the people in my family didn't know John because he was one of my best friends in high school who had a difficult life and died far too young. His room had been decorated the most simply of all. The truth was—with a life cut short—it was difficult to fill space with things he hadn't yet discovered about himself. So, I didn't try. Instead, I honored what I had known about him. He had loved baseball, was an amazing drummer and after high school served proudly as a Marine. He was a great brother and a tireless protector of all those he held close to him. His framed photograph was of the two of us the day he graduated high school. At one point he hadn't thought he would, and in that picture, I could still see one of the proudest moments of his life.

We headed back downstairs and into the sitting room when the room tour came to an end. We still had the others to get checked in once they arrived. My grandmother was the first to speak. "It's exactly what it should be, Paige," she said. I was sitting next to her, and she reached over and grabbed my hand. "You put your heart into this place. You put our hearts into this place, and there wasn't anyone who could have done it better. You have made me very proud."

I squeezed her hand back. "I just wanted to create something that told the story of our family. I wanted all of you to know what great support you have all given me throughout my life. How lucky I am to be a part of this family. And I didn't know any better way than showing you through the creation of all of this."

"Nancy, are you crying again?" my dad asked my mom. I looked over to where she was sitting, as she hastily wiped something from her eye.

"Be quiet, you. And no, I'm not crying again. I haven't stopped since the first room, so there," she said. The rest of us laughed. She joined in, and then swatted my father in the stomach.

CHAPTER FOURTEEN

An Affair To Remember

It was just after six thirty by the time we got everyone checked in, and the tours of the main house were complete. After the reveal of the rooms, all being a big hit, I was feeling pretty excited for the rest of the surprises that were to come for everyone. Ben, Holly, Grandma Rose, Grandpa Frank, Uncle Robert and Aunt Lynn had all arrived around the same time, followed shortly by Uncle Simon and Aunt Charlotte. We had given everyone about a half hour to get themselves settled and planned on meeting in the library at seven o'clock for cocktails and an overview of the night's events.

Once everyone made it downstairs, the first noticeable change was that all the gifts and packages that had accompanied everyone to the inn were now tucked safely under the tree in the library, waiting to be opened around the fire the next morning. This was the first Christmas that I could recall where we were all in one place for the holidays. I had originally hoped to get all the cousins to the inn as well, but because of the need for travel combined with the sort of last-minute confirmation that it would even be possible to host at Hummingbird Hollow, it wasn't meant to be. Maybe we would be able to make it happen the following year.

We got everyone settled and then Alice and I stood in front of the group so that we could address everyone. At first Emily, Jake, and Ben were resistant to joining the group, instead trying to stay and be extra hands for Alice and me. But since it was meant to be a gift to each of them as well, I remained stubborn until they gave in and agreed to join in on the fun.

"Thank you all for being here with us tonight, you have no idea how much it means to me that you have all made the trip to spend Christmas in this magical little inn that Grandma Jane has brought into our lives. Tonight, we have a couple of treats for you, including an amazing dinner by the brilliant and talented Alice," I gestured toward her with flourish, and she took an adorable little curtsy. "I'm sure you are all absolutely going to love everything she has prepared. Before dinner, however, we thought it might be nice to have a little entertainment while you sit by the fire and enjoy your cocktails." As I finished my sentence, a caroling sextet started walking in from the foyer. Each couple was dressed to the nines in full costume.

"I'd like to introduce you to the Dickens Carole's. Please, enjoy the show. Dinner will be ready in the main dining room at the conclusion of their performance."

"Oh my..." Grandma Rose said. I knew she was going to love this part of the program.

Alice and I quietly stepped out of the room in order to check on things in the dining room. Sasha, Taylor, and Marcus had already transformed the dining room into a beautiful winter night. Candles and sparkling centerpieces made the room feel like it had been part of a fresh snowfall. Each table setting had a name placard with frosted cranberries decorating them. "How can I help?" I started to ask at the same time Alice did a little dance.

"This is so much fun! Sasha, Taylor, Marcus, quick go quietly poke your head in the other room. If you get caught, use the cocktails as an excuse and offer to replenish them. You're going to love it!" Alice said, shooing her team away. I couldn't help it, I started to laugh. "As for you, all I need is for you to follow me into the kitchen and be my taste tester. I want to make sure I nailed the courses. Oh! That reminds me," Alice continued, waving at me to follow her into the kitchen.

"I know you usually do buffet style for Christmas Eve, but I thought it would be nicer if we plated the meal."

I thought about it for a minute, torn. While I did love the feel of an elegant plated meal, the variations to the food options didn't make it feel quite right. Alice noticed my hesitance. "No? Too much?"

"I like the idea for sure. I was just trying to figure out how it would work. Tomorrow's menu is better fit for a plated meal because there are less choices. But with all the different choices that could be made with tonight's meal, I'm just trying to imagine how that would work. What if we plated the appetizer and the salad courses, but then didn't plate the main course or desserts somehow? Would that work?" I asked. I wasn't trying to second guess Alice's vision, but she asked, and I wanted to be honest.

"Actually..." Alice started, and I could quickly see her mind redesigning the meal in front of my eyes. Finally, hers lit up and I knew she'd landed on the solution. "Yes. It'll be even more perfect. We'll plate appetizers and salad, like you said, and then we'll serve the pasta and the sausages and toppings family style on platters! We can bring the wine bottles out and leave them on the table and we can push the tables together to make one large table."

I smiled. "I love it," I said. "Put me to work," She had me go collect Marcus and Taylor to reconfigure the dining room with the new setup while Sasha finished refreshing the cocktails and then joined her in the kitchen to finish plating the first two courses. We could hear the concert winding down in the sitting room, so we knew we needed to move quickly.

Alice came into the dining room to approve the reconfigured table, and then gave the word for the first course to be brought out. "Paige, why don't you go get our guests. If they are finished with their drinks, have them leave their glasses in the library. I'll have the team take care of that room while everyone is eating their salads."

I nodded, whispered my thanks to all four of them once more for being with me and making sure everything was perfect and then headed into the library. "How did you all enjoy the music?" I asked as the Carole's filed out. I'd circle back and meet them in the foyer once I got everyone on their way to the dining room. Once the praise for the group died down, I continued. "If you have finished with your cocktails, please feel free to leave those here, and then please head this way and join us for dinner," I said, gesturing toward the dining room. Emily led the way since she knew where she was going, followed by Heidi, Holly and Ben, with the rest of the family right behind. I could hear the murmurs as everyone took in the décor and smiled.

I turned back to the foyer and found Jake waiting for me. "You are supposed to be heading in to eat," I said.

"So are you," he smiled back.

"I promise I'll be right there, I just need to thank the singers and then I'll be on my way."

"I'm happy to wait," he said, leaning up against the opening between the library and the foyer and taking another sip of his cocktail.

"You're impossible, you know," I said outwardly exasperated, but inwardly my stomach was doing a little happy dance. I turned and headed behind the front desk to grab the envelope with payment and a generous tip for each of the singers before Jake could see my cheeks catch fire once more.

When the Carolers were on their way, I headed back to where he stood waiting, and gave myself permission to admire him from afar for just a moment while he was occupied setting his cocktail glass gown. He was in dark jeans, that fit him well, and a cream shawl neck sweater. He looked amazing. He also turned and caught me looking, and my cheeks lit up once more when he smiled knowingly. "Ready for dinner?" he asked, graciously offering me his arm. He leaned over and whispered, "Have I mentioned you look beautiful tonight?"

While he had indeed already mentioned it, the impact was the same and my rebellious cheeks made the decision then and there to maintain a perpetual shade of pink for the remainder of the night. With nothing left to do, I accepted their fate and took Jake's arm.

We joined the rest of the family and found our chairs, Jake in between Ben and I with my mom on the other side of me. Emily and Heidi were across from us, and my grandmother sat at the head in between my father and Uncle Simon. Everyone had almost finished their appetizers by the time Jake and I sat down, so we ate ours while we listened to the family rave about them. Marcus came up behind us and asked which wine we'd prefer. Jake and I both opted for the red. Next up, the team brought our salads. Bright greens, pomegranate and pumpkin seeds made the food as pleasing to the eye as it was to the palate. Talking quieted down a little as people ate and drank, and before we knew it, the main course was being brought out. Taylor, Marcus, and Sasha continued to move effortlessly around the table, refilling glasses of wine and water, removing plates, and shifting utensils. Whatever was needed. It was a beautiful dance to watch as they did it in such a way that most of the family barely even registered what was happening. My dad caught me sitting back and taking everything in, and he reached out and squeezed my hand.

"You've given us quite the gift, Butter Bean," my dad whispered as he looked around and saw what I saw. Our family was the gift.

When dinner was finished and everyone had determined that not another bite could be consumed, my aunt turned to me and smiled. "We're all so stuffed. What should we do until we can make room for dessert?'

"Charades in the library," I responded simply, taking another sip of my wine.

"I'm in," my mom said, raising her hand.

"Do we get to pick our own teams?" My Uncle Derrick asked. "I want Ben and Jake if we do."

"No way! You can't put all three artists on the same team, that's cheating," Holly chimed in.

"You can be on it too," my uncle threw in, bribing her.

"Then yes, absolutely! I say we pick our own teams," Holly said raising her hand like my mom had done.

"I'm pretty great at drawing stick figures, you know," Grandpa Frank piped up laughing.

"Okay, okay. Before we all start campaigning for team members, I was hoping I could ask each of you to meet Emily and I in the foyer to retrieve your coats. We have something we'd like to show you outside before we get the game started." I nodded at Emily and she smiled as we both stood and walked out of the dining room.

"What are you two up to?" I heard my Grandma Rose say as we hurried to the coat closet and began pulling out everyone's coats.

"You'll see. Coat first," I said helping both of my grandmothers don their long winter coats and bundling their scarves around their necks. Once everyone else was appropriately outfitted for the night air, I opened the front door and stepped back, allowing everyone to step outside onto the porch. As they did, they saw a line of horse-drawn carriages awaiting them in the half-moon drive. There were ten total, enough for everyone. Once again, the drivers were decked out in Victorian Christmas garb, the horses whinnied and tossed their braided manes ready for their work to begin. As they moved around, the sound of sleigh bells whispered across the night air. It was magical.

"What is all this?" Grandma Jane asked, her eyes alight.

"It's our Christmas sleigh ride, Grandma. That first horse is Noelle, and she's been waiting for you," I whispered as I looked at my grandmother and saw the magic dance in her eyes. I turned toward the rest of the group and spoke a little louder. "There are blankets in each carriage, as well as a thermos filled with spiced cider that Alice has made from scratch for all of us. The drivers will take you on a tour of the Christmas lights and town Christmas tree before depositing you back here."

I headed down the stairs to the first of the carriages. The driver smiled and nodded, and Uncle Simon, Aunt Charlotte, and Grandma Jane made their way to the front. Once they were settled, the driver gave Noelle's reigns a little nudge and they were off. Next were Uncle Derrick and Aunt Charlotte, followed by my parents. And so on and so forth until all the carriages were full. As Emily and Heidi climbed into the final carriage, Emily told me to hop in with them. I shook my head. "Come with us," she said. "You deserve to enjoy this too!"

"That carriage is made for two. Go and enjoy! I'll be here when you get back and you can tell me all about it. I'm going to head inside and get my drawing fingers warmed up."

The driver nodded at me smiling and then gave the reigns a little shake and off they went into the night. I stayed put for a minute longer to listen as the sleigh bells drifted off into the distance and was just about ready to turn and head inside when I noticed another carriage pulling up from down the drive. I quickly did the math in my head to see if I'd forgotten anyone and realized Jake had disappeared at some point. As the driver pulled up, I found him sitting in the back of the carriage, wrapped in one of the blankets holding two cups of hot cider. He just smiled at me as the driver climbed down to help me into the carriage.

"It's a beautiful night for a carriage ride," Jake said. "I know you hadn't planned on joining in on this part of the evening, but I just couldn't let you miss out." He handed me my cup as I got into the carriage, and then lifted the blanket so I could climb underneath it as I sat. Once we were both tucked in, Jake waved to the porch where I saw Alice, Marcus, Sasha, and Taylor waving.

"I see you had help," I said laughing.

"I'm not ashamed to admit it. Cheers to a magical evening so far, with more to come," Jake said as he clinked my mug. "Thank you for inviting me to be a part of all of this. When Ben called two months ago and asked for my help, I had no idea it would lead to any of this," Jake turned so he was facing me, and his eyes held mine. "Listen Paige, I know you still have a lot of decisions to make once the inn gets open to the public, and your life is still a little in flux, but I need you to know that I plan on asking you out, officially, on a real date after Christmas. And I'm hoping you'll say yes."

I took another sip of my cider and looked around at the lights decorating the inn. The air was silent except for the sound of horse hooves and sleigh bells. I meant what I'd said when I told both Holly and Emily that I didn't have time to get involved with someone, but the truth that I'd been hiding in my heart—probably even from myself—was that there was never an ideal time. Life was always going to be busy. I was always going to have something else going on. What I did know was that I liked spending time with the man sitting beside me in a horse-drawn carriage on a cold Christmas night. I turned back to him, pretending to think about it once more.

"I might be open to saying yes," I said smiling. "What did you have in mind?"

Jake smiled and sat back looking around at all the lights on the inn. "Well, for now," he said taking my hand in his, "I think we just enjoy this carriage ride. But what are you doing New Years Eve?"

By the time we got back to the inn, the other carriages were parked in front of us and unloading. Jake squeezed my hand before letting it go, helping me up and the driver helping me down. "Thank you again, both of you," I said to them. "That was more beautiful than I could have expected." I quickly headed up the main steps to make sure I was there to let everyone in. The family filed back into the foyer where Emily and I took their coats once more and hung them up. As they chatted about the carriage rides, Emily leaned over and whispered, "I'm coming to your room tonight so you can fill me in on what just happened, missy," and then led everyone back into the library.

Alice came around the corner and met me at the reception desk. "We're talking on Monday. Until then, there is hot chocolate, more cider, and coffee waiting for everyone in the library."

"I thought you said you were heading out?" I asked, not expecting her to be there still.

"I did, and I am. Sasha, Marcus, Taylor, Ryan and Steve are all gone, and I'm making my departure now. The dining room is all setup for tomorrow night, and the breakfast buffet is staged just like we talked about."

"Thank you again, Alice, for everything. Tonight has been amazing," I said hugging her.

"You have no idea how much of a pleasure it was for me. Thank you for bringing me into this family, Paige. I cannot wait to see what we do next." She squeezed me tightly before letting me go. "Merry Christmas to you and your family!" she called, as she bundled herself up and headed out the front door.

"Drive safe! Text me to let me know you made it home! And Merry Christmas!" I called after her. I headed into the library where the game of charades had already begun with gusto.

The rest of the night was spent together, laughing and talking. We finally broke into the desserts which had also been brought into the library by way of a long thin table covered with red plaid linens. The amount of baking Alice had done was monumental, and everything that we tried was better than the last. We thought we were full after dinner, but that now felt like amateur hour. We hadn't really understood full until after dessert.

It was well past midnight by the time everyone headed to bed. Jake left, promising, like Alice, to text when he made it home. He didn't know it yet, but waiting for him in his truck would be his filled stocking and a five by seven red envelope with his name on it, thanks to my valet elves. I locked up the inn, heading upstairs with the others. The morning was going to come bright and early, and I was exhausted. I busied myself getting ready for bed until I heard nothing but silence from the rest of the rooms. Emily had changed her mind and decided we could have our girl talk later, as the excitement of the evening wore off and the long day also caught up with her. Once I was sure everyone was asleep, I headed back downstairs to get everything perfect for Christmas morning. When I did finally make it to my bed, I fell asleep quickly. It might have been short, but I was content, and I slept better than I had in quite a while.

CHAPTER FIFTEEN

Christmas Morning

'It's that time of year, when the world falls in love; every song you hear seems to say: Merry Christmas, may your New Year dreams come true; and this song of mine, in three-quarter time, wishes you and yours the same thing too...'

Pretty, I thought to myself. "I don't know how to waltz," I mumbled to Frank Sinatra... that could not be right. Consciousness began seeping in and I realized that my alarm was going off and Ol' Blue Eyes was nowhere to be found. I reached for my phone with my eyes still closed and silenced the alarm. I wanted to get up—really I did—but my eyes seemed to be mounting a full resistance to the thought of opening. They may be small, but boy are they fighters.

It took me a few minutes, but I finally regained control of my faculties, and while they were tearing up in rebellion, both eyelids finally did what they were born to do and opened. Once I could see, I looked around the room, bewildered for a minute. Where the heck was I? This was very much not my room. I felt the bedding around me. Nope, not my bed either. I had a minute of panic and felt my pajamas. Mine. Good, that was good. Hair, also mine. Face... a little dry but familiar nonetheless. I bet my rebel eyes were pretty proud of themselves right now, getting me all worked up and panicky. Then I remembered, this was not some sort of Dorothy waking up in Oz moment. I was at the inn. And if I was at the inn, then that meant it was... "CHRISTMAS!" I said loudly. Apparently, my vocal cords were proud to do their job this morning.

I sat up and threw my covers off of me. I'd set my alarm for 6:30a.m. hoping that I could get a little bit of sleep but still be the first one downstairs to get everything ready. I threw on my robe and slippers, brushed my hair back into a high bun, washed—and lotioned—my face, brushed my teeth and then headed downstairs.

The stockings for each family member were hung on the staircase and filled to the top with goodies from Santa. The presents were piled under the tree and the fireplace was ready to be lit. I started there, so that the room would have a chance to warm up. I then headed to the office under the stairs and got the basket of blankets I'd had ready for the morning's festivities and took those to the library as well. Then I headed to the front desk where I started the Christmas music playing, and finally padded off to the kitchen to get the coffee brewing and the pastries set out. As I rounded the corner, I heard soft talking coming from the kitchen letting me know that I had failed in my mission of being the first one up. I walked in quietly and saw my mom, aunt, uncle, and grandparents huddled around the island sipping coffee. I didn't want to interrupt since they looked like they were having a really nice moment together, so I snuck back out and headed up the last few stairs to come down again, this time with noise-filled gusto, revealing my eminent arrival to them.

My Uncle Robert was coming down the stairs as I played my little charade, and he smiled and let me have my moment before meeting me at the bottom. "Good morning, Paige, Merry Christmas," he said, kissing me on the top of my head. "Excellent performance, strong follow through, just one note: you turned on music, so chances are, they already know you're up and about," he said, heading into the kitchen.

Dang it. He was right. I followed him in and greeted everyone at the same time. "Merry Christmas! Did you all sleep okay?" I asked, heading to the coffee maker and pouring what remained of the first batch into two mugs, one for myself and the other for my uncle, and then started a new pot.

"We were just talking about that," my mom said, getting up to help me as she saw me starting to lay out the food. I was about to object, but then I realized that these small moments were just as important. My mom and I did this together every Christmas morning, and I loved it. "We slept great. Everything has been so amazing."

"You should be very proud, Paige," my grandpa said. "It was a lot of hard work, and you did an amazing job. We're so proud of you."

My Aunt Lynn got up and came over to help my mom and I. "After last night, I didn't think I'd ever be able to eat again..." she said, perusing the spread, "and yet..." she picked a tiny corner from a cream cheese danish and closed her eyes as she ate it. "This is really ridiculously good."

We all sat around in the kitchen for a little while longer, sipping hot coffee and laughing. It didn't take long to hear the stirrings of a house waking up, and the rest of the family started to make their way downstairs. As everyone came into the kitchen and greeted each other, grabbing their breakfast and drinks, I let them know to head into the smaller dining room to enjoy their breakfast. We would be heading back into the library soon, so that everyone could relax and sit comfortably while opening presents.

I slipped out and headed to the office under the stairs once more, grabbing the final surprise. A large red wrapped gift with a simple white bow. I placed it on top of the fireplace mantel in the library and then headed back to where everyone was eating.

When breakfast was done, everyone got refills on their hot beverage of choice, and started making their way to the library. I put my sister in charge of sorting the presents. It had been her duty for my entire life, and she was very efficient at it. Once everyone was seated and my sister had the presents identified and sorted, I walked over to the fireplace. I hadn't planned on making a speech but felt like a few words needed to be said. My entire family was here with me for the first time, and it was all to support this crazy little idea my grandmother had just two months ago. It meant the world to me, and I needed them to know that.

As I stood in front of the people who made me who I was at that very moment, I felt like I finally truly understood all those sappy writers who talked about family being the most precious gift. It was. The best gift. I quietly said a prayer of gratitude—and a happy birthday—to the Lord before starting.

"Hi," I said, suddenly feeling a little nervous. "Merry Christmas, everyone. Before we get started on this present-opening extravaganza, I just wanted to take a second to again say thank you for being here with me yesterday and today. I know I sound like a broken record, but I am just really grateful. And to Grandma Jane," I said looking at her and smiling. "Thank you for giving me this frustrating, stressful, all consuming, beautiful, and fulfilling project. I know there were days where we thought we would never make it, but we did. It's really because of all of you that we get to be here.

"To Emily, who saddled up and rode right alongside me through the adventure, and to Ben who kept this whole thing on the rails and taught me things I never even knew I needed to learn. Mom and Dad, thank you for putting up with me each and every day. For knowing when to push, and when to coddle, to keep me going. And to the rest of you, Uncle Derrick, for that amazing sign, Grandma and Grandpa, for your wisdom, Uncle Robert and Aunt Lynn... Holly... the memories made throughout this entire experience are ones that I will treasure forever. You guys are the best.

"Now, there is one more person who has made a pretty incredible contribution to this inn, and I thought now might be a great time to show him off to you a little bit. I'm not sure how many of you have heard, but Hummingbird Hollow has a resident artist who will be creating amazing and unique keepsakes for every single one of our guests. I know most of you have not seen his work, but I can say without a doubt that it is absolutely exquisite. I believe it will be one of the personal touches that will allow this inn to stand out in the mind of our patrons.

"I did think about having our artist create each of you a version of what our guests will receive, and in fact, did just that for the team that was here last night that couldn't join us today. For the family, however, he had something a little more special in mind. So, as a gift from Hummingbird Hollow to each of you..." I turned and unwrapped the large frame that I had set earlier on the fireplace, walking over to Grandma Jane and laying it on her lap. "Merry Christas, everyone. This family portrait will hang above the fireplace for all of our guests to see, because each of you are a part of this place."

My grandmother looked down at the charcoal sketched drawing of all of us together in front of the inn, fully decorated for Christmas. In the background were hints of horse-drawn carriages and Christmas trees. The attention to detail was unmatched. Even the matting around the sketch told a story. From a distance it looked like a simple texture design, but up close he had meticulously woven the names of family members who had passed on, creating a vein-like support structure around the sketch itself.

I watched as each of my family members studied the portrait in amazement, the room silent except for the crackling of the fireplace. Their eyes filled with tears, the exact way mine had the first time I'd seen the work of art. When everyone had finished, I handed it to my dad and his brothers. "Would you three kindly do the honors?" They held the frame carefully, trying to figure out what to do next. "Don't worry, Ben and Jake prepared for this moment, you'll see the hole ready for you right there," I said pointing and handing my dad a nail.

"Well, that's handy," my Uncle Simon said laughing. "You really did think of everything here."

"Don't you dare drop that, Charles," my mom said, making everyone join in on the laughter. Once the portrait was hung in its rightful spot, we all admired it for a few more moments.

"Okay, who's first?" My sister said grinning and holding up a package. "Let's get this show on the road!" Again, the room filled with laughter. "I'm just sayin'," she said, shrugging.

I went to sit down next to Emily and my Aunt Lynn, as my grandpa put one of his boxes on his head and pretended he could telepathically determine what was inside. Surprisingly over the years, he'd even been right a few times. As everyone watched him, I looked around the room that had been empty and cold the first time I entered it. I'd had no idea back then what the journey that took place between that moment, and the one I was now in, was going to look like—or how it would change my life. I hadn't known it would teach me the things I'd learned or bring the wonderful people it brought into my life. I thought of Alice and Jake. Of David, and all the new staff members and I smiled. I never knew that on Christmas morning I would be looking around that same exact room and have it feel like a part of my heart. That room, that inn, had become a living, breathing member of our family, and I found myself eternally grateful that it too could be there with all of us on Christmas morning.

I looked over to my Grandma Jane sitting between her eldest and youngest sons, one hand on each as she met my gaze. Her look was one filled with knowing, and she smiled and gave me wink. She, it turned out, had known all along.

Milton Keynes UK
Ingram Content Group UK Ltd.
UKHW021503301024
450479UK00012B/300

9 781962 715058